Murder of Cecily Thane

A Spike Tracy Mystery

By H. Ashbrook

Originally published in 1937

Murder of Cecily Thane

Published by Resurrected Press

This classic book was handcrafted by Resurrected Press. Resurrected Press is dedicated to bringing high quality classic books back to the readers who enjoy them. These are not scanned versions of the originals, but, rather, quality checked and edited books meant to be enjoyed!

Please visit ResurrectedPress.com to view our entire catalogue!

For updates on future releases, LIKE us on Facebook:
http://www.Facebook.com/ResurrectedPress

ISBN 13: 978-1-943403-16-5

Printed in the United States of America

RESURRECTED PRESS BOOKS IN
H. ASHBROOK'S
SPIKE TRACY MYSTERY SERIES

RESURRECTED PRESS CLASSIC
MYSTERY CATALOGUE

J. S. Fletcher
The Herapath Property
The Rayner-Slade Amalgamation
The Chestermarke Instinct
The Paradise Mystery
Dead Men's Money
The Middle of Things
Ravensdene Court
Scarhaven Keep
The Orange-Yellow Diamond
The Middle Temple Murder
The Tallyrand Maxim
The Borough Treasurer
In the Mayor's Parlour
The Saftey Pin

R. Austin Freeman
The Mystery of 31 New Inn from the Dr. Thorndyke Series
John Thorndyke's Cases from the Dr. Thorndyke Series
The Red Thumb Mark from The Dr. Thorndyke Series
The Eye of Osiris from The Dr. Thorndyke Series
A Silent Witness from the Dr. John Thorndyke Series
The Cat's Eye from the Dr. John Thorndyke Series
Helen Vardon's Confession: A Dr. John Thorndyke Story
As a Thief in the Night: A Dr. John Thorndyke Story
Mr. Pottermack's Oversight: A Dr. John Thorndyke Story
Dr. Thorndyke Intervenes: A Dr. John Thorndyke Story
The Singing Bone: The Adventures of Dr. Thorndyke
The Stoneware Monkey: A Dr. John Thorndyke Story
The Great Portrait Mystery, and Other Stories: A Collection of Dr. John Thorndyke and Other Stories
The Penrose Mystery: A Dr. John Thorndyke Story

The Uttermost Farthing: A Savant's Vendetta

Arthur Griffiths
The Passenger From Calais
The Rome Express

Fergus Hume
The Mystery of a Hansom Cab
The Green Mummy
The Silent House
The Secret Passage

Edgar Jepson
The Loudwater Mystery

A. E. W. Mason
At the Villa Rose

A. A. Milne
The Red House Mystery

Baroness Emma Orczy
The Old Man in the Corner

Edgar Allan Poe
The Detective Stories of Edgar Allan Poe

Arthur J. Rees
The Hampstead Mystery
The Shrieking Pit
The Hand In The Dark
The Moon Rock
The Mystery of the Downs

Mary Roberts Rinehart
Sight Unseen and The Confession

Dorothy L. Sayers

Whose Body?

Sir William Magnay
The Hunt Ball Mystery

Mabel and Paul Thorne
The Sheridan Road Mystery

Louis Tracy
The Strange Case of Mortimer Fenley
The Albert Gate Mystery
The Bartlett Mystery
The Postmaster's Daughter
The House of Peril
The Sandling Case: What Would You Have Done?

Charles Edmonds Walk
The Paternoster Ruby

John R. Watson
The Mystery of the Downs
The Hampstead Mystery

Edgar Wallace
The Daffodil Mystery
The Crimson Circle

Carolyn Wells
Vicky Van
The Man Who Fell Through the Earth
In the Onyx Lobby
Raspberry Jam
The Clue
The Room with the Tassels
The Vanishing of Betty Varian
The Mystery Girl
The White Alley
The Curved Blades

Anybody but Anne
The Bride of a Moment
Faulkner's Folly
The Diamond Pin
The Gold Bag
The Mystery of the Sycamore
The Come Back

Raoul Whitfield
Death in a Bowl

And much more!
Visit ResurrectedPress.com
for our complete catalogue

FOREWORD

The Murder of Cecily Thane is the first in a series of seven mystery novels by Harriette Ashbrook featuring the amateur sleuth Phillip (Spike) Tracy. Ashbrook was a member of that school of mystery writers who looked upon murder as an entertainment in contrast to the "hard-boiled" writers of detective fiction such as Dashiell Hammett, John Carroll Daly, and Raymond Chandler. The style had been popularized in America by the writers S.S. Van Dine, Ellery Queen and Rex Stout, and in Britain by writers such as Anthony Berkeley. These mysteries are more concerned with antics and wit of their detectives than they are with the sordid details of crime, in particular, the ability of their amateur sleuths to twit the official police who are often portrayed as bumbling dim-wits. Murder, when it occurs, mostly happens off-stage and with a minimum of blood and gore.

The detective of the series, Phillip Tracy, though he prefers to be called Spike, is the younger brother of the district attorney of New York, a relationship that provides him with ready access to crime. Spike is something of a feckless playboy with a tendency for being arrested for being "drunk and disorderly," a source of endless embarrassment for his more responsible elder brother. Of course, this character flaw doesn't prevent him from solving crimes that leave the more established police completely baffled.

Despite, or perhaps because of, his irresponsible personality, Spike Tracy is an engaging character. Unlike S.S. Van Dine's Philo Vance, he doesn't come off as an arrogant know-it-all of as oddly eccentric as Rex Stout's Nero Wolfe. Instead, beneath Spike's jaunty exterior, there is a caring and compassionate character, one who is truly interested in seeing justice done.

Spike's long suffering brother Richard and Detective Inspector Herschman of the Homicide Squad serve as convenient foils to Spike's humor and repartee. His brother, the D.A. is serious and sober, sorely lacking a sense of humor, and more interested in his political future than solving crimes, while Herschman is a quintessential New York policeman, honest and competent in an ordinary sort of way, but not overly endowed with either culture or intelligence. Yet, despite the fact that they serve as targets of Spike's wit, neither is portrayed as either fools or bumbling.

The mystery in *The Murder of Cecily Thane* is the murder of a well-off woman approaching middle-age. She is found murdered in her bedroom after a night in which she has gone out dancing with a paid escort. She is the apparent victim of a robbery, as she has been shot and several hundred thousand dollars worth of jewelry is missing. Her dancing partner of the evening is the immediate suspect, but motives and opportunities soon surface for a number of other suspects.

Of interest is the way Ashbrook deals with the subject of gigolos, the young men employed by older women of means to escort them to night clubs and social functions in place of their husbands. This seems to have been a institution peculiar to during the Depression when work of any sort was hard and a man would do anything to survive. While the treatment isn't completely sympathetic, it is at least understanding. Ashbrook's willingness to address social and moral issues is one of the things that set her apart from other mystery writers of the period.

Reading the Spike Tracy mysteries, it's hard to understand how they have become so neglected. The writing is crisp and the pace is quick. The elements of the mystery, while not necessarily innovative, are handled in a manner competent and fair enough to leave any reader satisfied. The character of Spike is likeable and his foils—his brother and Inspector Herschman—

handled at least as well as their counterparts in the Philo Vance or Nero Wolfe books. More importantly, despite their levity, there is some real substance to the novels. Yet despite all this, unfortunately the works of Ashbrook have languished in obscurity.

It is therefore with great pleasure that Resurrected Press offers this new edition of *The Murder of Cecily Thane* and the other books in the Spike Tracy series.

About the Author

Harriette Cora Ashbrook (1898-1946) was the American author of thirteen mystery novels. Seven of these were published under her own name and feature Phillip (Spike) Tracy, a playboy turned amateur sleuth whose brother just happens to be the District Attorney of New York. She also published six more mysteries under the pen-name Susannah Shane featuring Christopher Saxe as the detective.

Greg Fowlkes
Editor-In-Chief
Resurrected Press
www.ResurrectedPress.com

TABLE OF CONTENTS

I. X Marks the Spot!

"THERE are times, my dear brother, when I wonder why God lets you live."

As the district attorney paced in angry strides up and down the length of his office, his hands jammed into his pockets, he presented a severe contrast to the young man before him.

Slouched comfortably in a huge leather chair, one leg swinging nonchalantly over an upholstered arm, the young man blew long, lazy clouds of cigarette smoke into the air. A smile played about his lips, and the spring sunshine coming in through the open window bathed him with a pleasant, easy warmth, that seemed to match his disposition. He was gay and debonair despite the crumpled state of his Tuxedo and his obvious need of a shave.

"I repeat—there are times when I wonder why God lets you live and breathe and get into trouble."

"And this, I suppose, is one of them?" The young man spoke with the lazy indolence of great bodily ease and infinite amusement.

"Exactly!"

"Well, thank God, God isn't consulting you about the way He runs the universe."

"If you *must* get arrested, why not do it in some place beside New York? Paris—London—*anywhere* but here?"

"I have. Four times in Paris and three in London. Or, perhaps, it was the other way round. By the way, what was the name of the place where I bided the night?"

"Forty-seventh Precinct Station House."

"Not very interesting, is it? Still—" He drew a small black notebook and a pencil from his inner pocket and made an entry. "I'm keeping a list of the jails I've been in," he explained. "Perhaps some day I'll write a book— 'Jails I Have Known.' It'll be frightfully amusing. In Munich they serve champagne and put it on your bill. Once in Paris—"

"Stop that nonsense and try to take this thing seriously."

"But why?"

"Why? Because every damned paper in the town will be carrying the story on the front page."

"Really?" The young man grinned. "A member of the front page elite at last. Do you suppose they'd like my picture? Or maybe both of us together. I know—a passionate one for the tabs like this." He sprang from the chair and prostrated himself before the glare of his brother, his face hidden in his hands, his shoulders drooping with synthetic shame.

"'District Attorney Plays Erring Kin'"

"Look here, Philip," the older man's voice softened helplessly and he stopped his angry pacing. His tone was almost pleading. "If you can't take this thing seriously for yourself, look at it from my point of view. I'm supposed to be the public prosecutor here, to stand for law and order and decency, and my brother, my own brother gets run in on a charge of being drunk and disorderly."

"Well, what would you prefer—spitting in the subway or murder?"

At the last word the district attorney winced. "Don't talk about murder. I've got enough of it on my hands just now without a young ass like you adding to it in a jolly spirit of fun."

"Yeah?" The young man rose slowly from his ridiculous posture and dusted off his knees. "You mean you've got a murder on the pan right now?"

The district attorney nodded. "I was on my way up to the scene of the crime when I had to go chasing off after you and get you out of jail. Of all the times to get into trouble, you couldn't have picked a worse one, you couldn't have—"

"Really, old thing, there's nothing to be gained by going over all that again. And anyway, I think it would be much more interesting to talk about your murder."

"'My murder' is quite right. It probably will be." The district attorney became slightly calmer and much more gloomy. Then he burst out once more in sudden irritation. "Why did this have to come just now when I'm working on the state banking laws? The newspapers make such a fuss about murders. This sort of thing," and he indicated a copy of the morning paper on his desk, folded at the editorial page.

The young man picked it up and read the paragraph indicated by his brother's vehement finger.

"The present police and legal administration may seek to camouflage successive failures with grandiloquent talk of 'civic progress' and 'worthy reforms,' but the man in the street is not deceived by such high-sounding phrases. The fact remains that since District Attorney Tracy has been in office there have been three unsolved murders to his discredit. As an officer of the people, pledged to the punishment of those who transgress the law, it seems to us that he has been flagrantly unsuccessful in the discharge of his duty. A little bit more effective criminal investigation and fewer, 'worthy reforms' would do much to redeem his administration. 'Reform' like charity should begin at home."

The young man laid down the paper.

"It strikes me," he said, "that that fellow doesn't like you."

"'Doesn't like me?' They're just waiting for an opportunity to get me. Damn the newspapers! If there isn't something new to tell them each day, they make up something that is usually worse than the truth and they—"

"There, there," the young man broke in soothingly. "Tell me all and get it off your chest and then you'll feel better. Who killed whom and where and what and why?"

"Cecily Thane."

"Cecily Thane?" He opened his eyes with sudden interest.

"You know her?"

"No, I can't say that I know her. I've seen her around in night clubs a good deal and of course every one knows about her jewels."

"Well, she's dead—murdered last night—and $200,000 worth of jewels are missing from her private wall safe." The district attorney turned and with sudden belligerence shot a question at his brother. "What do *you* know about it, anyway?"

"Now, now, Richard, my pet, I didn't do it, I swear I didn't and if you don't believe it ask the excellent sergeant and the two patrolmen down at the police station who played poker with me all night."

"I mean what do you know about *her?*"

"Just gossip. She's always seen about with some young fellow, usually sporting about three pecks of diamonds. They say they don't all belong to her, but that she takes 'em out of her husband's store. They call her the walking showcase."

"Well, she's dead and I can't fool any more time talking about it. I've got to find out who killed her. Just my luck."

"Mine too." The young man reached for his hat and stick lying on the desk.

"What do you mean, 'yours' too?"

"I mean that I was going up to British Columbia and hunt elk, but now I think I'll stay here in New York and hunt murderers instead. Much better sport."

He put on his hat and motioned toward the door.
"Come!"

"Come where?"

"To the X which always marks the spot where the
body's found."

It was difficult to believe that R. Montgomery Tracy,
known officially to the bar as the district attorney of New
York County, was the brother of Philip Tracy, that
insouciant young man who, under the more familiar
name of Spike enlivened existence on both sides of the
Atlantic.

The marital difficulties of the late R. Montgomery
Tracy, Sr., and his wife, may to a degree have accounted
for the divergence in the two sons. It was soon after
Philip was born that Mrs. Tracy, always of a flighty
disposition, refused point-blank to languish longer under
the stern Puritan rule of her husband. Forthwith, she
picked up her youngest child and went to Europe,
becoming soon a part of that irresponsible, delightful
European population that rotates from St. Moritz to the
Riviera, to Paris, with an occasional visit to London or
Berlin.

Philip had grown up a charming hybrid, half
American, half continental, a pleasing combination of
Piccadilly and Broadway, Oxford and Yale, dividing his
time between school in France and England, and visits to
his father and older brother in America.

He had not confused the issues of his existence with
anything so dismal as a profession. College was a
pleasant interlude between boyhood and manhood—an
interlude of failures in the classroom and triumphs on the
athletic field and the prom floor. Inability to graduate
brought only a joyous feeling of release into a world that
was waiting for a playboy—Paris, New York, Vienna. His
twenty-five years had been lived with a gay intensity
made possible by the unceasing flow of dollars from the

paternal estate. His life was utterly useless and infinitely amusing.

Yet this could not be considered an entirely accurate estimate of him. When the occasion demanded he could display a shrewdness that seemed at complete variance with his more apparent character. There lay underneath his facetious exterior, a quickness of perception that sometimes puzzled those who surprised him in the occasional exercise of it.

But his brother was not among them.

At forty R. Montgomery Tracy had a wife and four children, political ambitions, and a sense of humor so rudimentary as to be practically nonexistent. Many years of contact with the majesty of the law had imparted to him a certain depressing heaviness that at times clouded the sharpness of his vision when dealing with less abstract human factors. Life, be felt, was not to be taken lightly.

As district attorney of New York County he displayed a dogged efficiency that was at once the pride and the despair of his supporters. He served with the fearless honesty commanded only by a man whose inheritance puts him above financial temptation. There were many solid achievements to his regime of which his followers could boast.

But on the more spectacular side he was lacking. Already there were rumblings of disapproval at his failure to provide a good show for the masses. Of bread he gave them plenty but he was a poor ringmaster for their circuses.

For murders particularly he had an intense distaste. They interfered so with the solid constructive program which he in his unimaginative way believed would lead him on to higher and nobler political heights. They precipitated mobs of reporters into his office and brought a thrill-thirsty public howling about his ears.

And now here was another one on his hands—a gaudy, spectacular one. Elton Thane's sudden rise to fame as a jewel merchant had been broadcast throughout the success journals of the country. Ten years ago a salesman—now a millionaire. Importer of rare and precious gems which once had adorned the now defunct crowns of Europe. Owner of a costly shop on the Avenue and of a smaller branch uptown in the eighties on Broadway.

The district attorney shuddered to think of the afternoon papers. As he rode north on Lafayette with his younger brother toward a certain house in West Eighty-second Street, the argument which had begun at Police Headquarters was still in progress.

"But, my dear boy," he protested, "I refuse to permit you to make a Roman holiday out of the most serious crime in the penal code."

"But I'm not. I'm going to apply myself to the serious study of a serious crime and I shouldn't be surprised if I found it not too boring."

"In other words, you're fancying yourself in the role of a detective?"

"Well, something of the sort."

For the first time that morning the district attorney laughed.

"Herschman will enjoy that."

"Who's Herschman?"

"In charge of the Homicide Squad."

"And when will I have the pleasure of his acquaintance?"

"In about fifteen minutes. He's up there now."

"Oh, so you *are* going to take me with you?" Tripped up in the unsuspecting web of his own making the district attorney considered.

"Well, just this morning. You may come with me to the house but please don't bother with nonsensical questions. Make yourself as unobtrusive as possible."

"A sort of unofficial observer."

"Exactly. And try to look slightly serious. Remember a woman has been killed."

"Oh, absolutely!" and Spike grinned.

II. Spike Makes an Utter Damn Fool of Himself

THE home of Elton Thane at 8 West Eighty-second Street was one of a row of brownstone fronts, dreary of exterior, but with a certain smartness in the shine of brass knockers and the glisten of well-washed windows that bespoke servants and money. Standing on the south side of the street just three doors to the west of Central Park West, it was a victim of the terrific din which accompanied the building of the Eighth Avenue subway which at that time was in process of construction.

The pavement of Central Park West was torn up, and what traffic was forced through it, bumped and jolted perilously over the rutted roadbed. Timbered shafts had been sunk at intervals, and men could be glimpsed working twenty or thirty feet below the surface. At Eighty-second Street, the site of a prospective station, the street was laid open as if by a great gouging fist and in the excavation men worked with electric drills, boring away at a stubborn rock formation.

Emerging from the transverse concourse of the Park at Seventy-second Street, the automobile carrying the district attorney and his brother picked its way carefully northward, threading in and out among supply trucks and cement mixers. At Eighty-second Street its occupants were forced to get out and walk the short distance from the corner to Number 8, for the station excavation was at its widest directly in front of the Thane house, closing the street to traffic from the east.

"Ideal spot for a murder, isn't it?" Spike spoke above the din of the drills.

The district attorney frowned in disapproval and
started up the steps, but a restraining hand was laid on
his arm.

"Really, old thing," Spike protested, "do you think
you're approaching the problem just the right way? Isn't
it always customary to stop and observe?"

"Observe?"

"You know—footprints on the doormat and
automobile tracks and all that."

"There is no doormat and automobiles don't make
tracks on asphalt."

"Well then, shouldn't something be done about those
men?" and Spike indicated the workmen in the station
excavation. "We at least ought to stop and note the color
of their eyes and whether they have been vaccinated and
how long since—"

"Philip!" the district attorney thundered, but it was a
hushed thunder out of respect to the dead within. "Philip,
I refuse to permit such levity. Either you drop your
facetious manner or you leave me on the threshold."

"Why, Richard, I was merely trying to be helpful."

"Well, don't. The legal and police departments can
handle this case without any assistance from a man who
has just spent the night in jail."

Spike acquiesced meekly, but out of the corner of his
eye he cast a furtive glance at the workmen—three
sweating little Italians and a huge foreman with fierce
black whiskers. He looked like pictures of a Russian
Nihilist but his voice as he ordered the three little men
about was unmistakably tinged with an Irish brogue.

At the top of the steps a policeman standing guard
saluted respectfully and opened the door for the district
attorney and his companion.

The door gave on to a small vestibule, and this in turn
on to a long hall along the right of which rose a flight of
stairs to the second floor. The interior of the Thane house
was in marked contrast to its conventional façade. As the
two men stepped over the threshold, they were assaulted

by a flaring mass of color from green and mauve walls and vermilion hangings. Chairs of uneven architecture, tables at varying levels, bookcases holding futuristic statuettes instead of books, lighting fixtures concealed behind strangely angled pieces of glass. Bizarre, unrestful. Obviously the late Mrs. Thane had gone in for the newer things in decoration.

To the left was a wide arched opening into the drawing room, from which came a low hum of voices. Inspector Herschman and one of his men were seated rather incongruously on a triangular divan with three legs of perilous thinness.

Any reader of detective fiction would at once have recognized Herschman for what he was—a Headquarters dick. In face and form and haberdashery he conformed exactly to the popular idea of what a Headquarters dick should be. A massive fellow with that certain rough capability that comes of a long apprenticeship at pavement pounding in a city whose population is crowded into a space only half large enough for comfort. One could easily imagine him cowing a bunch of gangsters. But it was more difficult to picture him pitted against a Raffles or a Steinlin.

He looked a trifle ruefuly at the district attorney as if to remind him of his long delay in arriving at the scene of the crime. But Tracy made no explanation of the fraternal difficulties which had entangled him, and introduced Spike as briefly as possible.

"My brother. He just happened to be with me this morning so I brought him along."

Then nervously he got down to business. "Let me have a brief summary of the whole situation. I know only the bare outline of the case as you told it to me this morning on the telephone." And Herschman went ahead with his explanation.

Shortly before four o'clock that morning, Elton Thane had returned home and started up to his room on the third floor. Noticing a light in the sitting room of his wife's apartment on the second floor, he had knocked. Receiving no answer he walked in and discovered her body. She had been shot through the heart. Her jewels had been torn from her throat and her private wall safe had been emptied of $200,000 worth of diamonds, emeralds and pearls.

"The body hasn't been removed yet from the room upstairs," Herschman said, "and everything is just as we found it. I thought you'd probably want a look before anything was disturbed."

Tracy nodded approval and the inspector continued.

Elton Thane had immediately summoned a Dr. Partridge, a friend and physician, who lived next door, who had in turn called the police at the Eighty-sixth Street Station. After a preliminary survey of the situation, Groaty and McCarthy, the detectives who had answered the call, reported to Headquarters, and Herschman had himself personally taken charge of the case. Firearms and fingerprint men had already been there and Sayler, the medical examiner, was upstairs making his examination before the body was removed.

"Any leads?" Tracy inquired nervously.

"Well, I've got Groaty and McCarthy out looking for the man Mrs. Thane went out with last night. A chap named Spencer, Tommy Spencer. The two of them— Spencer and Mrs. Thane left the house last night about eight o'clock, bound for some dancing place. At eleven-thirty they came home and went up to Mrs. Thane's apartment on the second floor. About a half hour later he left."

Tracy was thoughtful for a moment. Then his gaze met that of Herschman and each nodded as if confirming the other's thought.

"It has a number of points of similarity with the Schlockenhass case," the district attorney said.

"Yeah. So many that I told Groaty and McCarthy to take a look at the photographs and fingerprints in that case before they started their hunt."

"Have you a description of the jewels missing?"

"Not yet. The husband, the only one that knows anything about them, is so busted up that he hasn't been able to talk yet."

"Well, suppose we go upstairs."

As the three men mounted the stairs—the district attorney and Herschman leading and Spike trailing in their wake, the very picture of meekness and unofficial observation—the Inspector outlined the general plan of the house. In common with most brownstone fronts it had four stories and a basement with three rooms on each floor. The kitchen and furnace room took up the entire length of the basement with the exception of a small room in front made into a sitting room for the servants. A small door and two iron-barred windows opened from the sitting room directly on to the street. At the back was a door from the kitchen opening on to a small grass plot surrounded completely by a high brick wall.

On the first floor was the dining room, drawing room and at the back a small bedroom and bath. The second floor was Mrs. Thane's apartment, consisting of a bedroom and bath and sitting room. And on the floor above, Mr. Thane had similar quarters. The three bedrooms on the fourth floor were occupied by the maid, and the cook and the butler.

"I suppose you have questioned them all?" Tracy asked.

"Only the maid. She was the only one who was home last night. It was the cook's night off and she was visiting friends in Jersey, and the butler left yesterday."

"That's unfortunate," the district attorney said. "When you have more than one story to go by it is easier to piece together the real one."

The second floor of the Thane house bore further evidence of the variety in interior decorating taste of its late occupant. The sitting room was done more or less in the style of Louis XIV with small gold-legged chairs, a Fragonard carpet, paneled walls and 'taffeta drapery in billowing loops of shirring. A doll dressed as a college flapper struck an ungainly note as it sprawled among the pillows of a chaise longue copied after the famous Récamier portrait.

To the right as the three men entered the sitting room from the hall was a wide archway leading to the bedroom whence came incongruously enough whistled snatches of a gay, lilting popular song. Dr. Sayler, official medical examiner of the New York police force, was seated in apparent contentment on a gold lacquered chair, in the bedroom, whiling away the time whistling and smoking, unmoved apparently by the lugubriousness of his surroundings.

"The inspector told me you were coming," he called cheerily to the district attorney, "so I stayed around a bit. Thought you might like to see exactly how things lie before I removed the body."

With an airy gesture he indicated the corner of the room directly to the right of the archway, leading from the sitting room to the bedroom.

Cecily Thane lay on her back, one arm thrown upward over her head, her mouth slightly open. She was a woman at that tragic, indeterminate age, somewhere between thirty-five and forty-five. At one time she must have been beautiful but with an ephemeral blond beauty that had begun to fade early. The hair, geometrically waved was just a shade too blond, and the thin angularity of her face was heightened by triangular spots of rouge under prominent cheek bones. The lips were thin, drawn tightly into a scarlet penciled line. The whole face bore a look of chronic strain, of nervous tension that could not be attributed entirely to whatever strange and terrifying events had immediately preceded the tragedy.

She was wearing an evening gown of opaline satin heavily encrusted with sequins. Over the left breast an ugly spot of red spread out through the glittering cloth.

On the wall about five feet from the baseboard, a wall safe stood open; and scattered about the floor were several small jewel boxes and one larger one with trays. Boxes and safe were empty. The body lay directly in front of the safe, about three feet from the wall.

The district attorney looked inquiringly at the medical examiner.

"It must have occurred some time about twelve or shortly after," he said. "Certainly not after one o'clock. A clean shot directly through the heart."

He stepped over to the body and with the unconcern of a laboratory lecturer, demonstrated. "You can see there are no powder burns. Probably fired at a distance of three or four feet. The bullet entered the body here just to the left of the breastbone."

"Have you the bullet?"

The doctor shook his head. "No, it came out just to the left of the backbone. I suppose one of your men picked it up, Inspector?"

"I have it here," Herschman replied. "It's from a .38 caliber Colt. About the commonest type of gun there is."

Walking to a point on the south side of the bedroom he indicated a spot in the paneling of the wall, just below one of the large windows that gave on to the rear of the house. "You can see the spot here where it hit."

Dr. Sayler, the district attorney and Spike crowded around the inspector to examine the small dent about one-fourth of an inch deep which the bullet had made in the soft painted wood of the paneling

"Well, suppose we have the maid up," Tracy said "I'd like to go over her story with her."

Herschman gave an order to one of the officers whom he had stationed just outside the door of the sitting room and presently a buxom, slightly pretty young woman of perhaps twenty-five appeared from below stairs. Her name, Emma Bloomstead, should have indicated a Scandinavian stolidity, an harassing inarticulateness, but she belied it. She was of the second generation of immigrants and she talked freely. Obviously shaken by the events of the previous night, she was also obviously impressed with her own role in the official limelight

"How long have you been employed in this household?" Tracy began his questioning

"About five years."

"And you were the only one of the servants in the house last night?"

"Yes, sir."

"Now, Emma," Tracy went on, using an entirely unnecessary propitiatory tone. "I want you to tell us just exactly what happened last night as well as you can remember it."

"Well, Mrs. Thane went out about eight with Mr. Spencer like she does quite often and—"

"You mean Mr. Spencer is a good friend, comes here often?"

"Twice a week, on Monday and Thursdays, and they always go out together. He must have lots of money because she always dresses up swell in evening gowns like she was going to swell places Well, last night about eight she goes out with him and she tells me they'll be back about eleven-thirty, which is sort of early because usually it's one and two and three and sometimes four when they get home.

"Well, then I came upstairs and sort of straightened things up up here, hung up dresses, and emptied the ash trays, and put away shoes and things, and then I went downstairs and pretty soon Mr. Thane rings for me and sends me down to the corner to mail a letter. And a little while later when I got back he went out, about nine o'clock.

"And then about eleven-thirty, Mrs. Thane and Mr. Spencer got back, and they rang for me to bring up some ice and vichy and I did."

"You mean up here in the sitting room?" the district attorney interrupted.

"Yes, sir, right in this room. I came up with the stuff on a tray and there was Mrs. Thane sitting over there on that chaise longue and Mr. Spencer sort of ranging around the room waiting till he could get his hands on a cocktail shaker. And so I left the tray there and went downstairs again."

"Downstairs? You mean to the first floor?"

"No, to the servants' sitting room in the basement. Then a little while later, after I had taken the tray up to the sitting room, the bell in the first floor front hall rings and there is Mr. Spencer wanting his hat and stick and I gave them to him and he left."

"How did he seem—nervous or hurried?"

"Not a bit of it. As calm as a cucumber. And took his time about things. Tried to joke a little bit with me but I didn't let him get away with it. No good ever comes of mixing with the mistress' boy friends."

"Does Mr. Thane know—know of this Mr. Spencer?" Tracy inquired with a significant inflection.

"Knows him and talks right friendly with him too. Why only last night when Mr. Spencer comes to call for Mrs. Thane, he meets him downstairs in the front parlor and they have me bring up the seltzer bottle and the Scotch, and there they were drinking a highball together just as chummy as you please."

"You don't by any chance recall any of the conversation which you overheard between them?"

The maid pondered for a moment, reaching into the recesses of her memory for any stray bits of talk.

"Well, they weren't talking about anything much. Just talking like men do, you know. Mr. Thane had a new golf club he was showing off and he was near busting up everything in the place, swinging it around. And then by-and-by Mrs. Thane came down and the three of them just stood there and talked for a minute or so; and then I heard Mr. Thane tell 'em to be home early just like she was his daughter instead of his wife, and Mr. Spencer said yes, they'd be home about eleven-thirty."

The maid sniffed. It was plain that she did not approve of the complacent attitude of her employer. He was not acting up to her standards of an outraged husband.

"To continue with your story—Mr. Spencer rang for his hat and stick and you gave them to him. And then what?"

"He left and I went on back downstairs."

"Do you remember what time it was?"

"Yes, sir. It was just about a minute after twelve. I looked at the clock especially because Mr. Thane had always told me to sit up until twelve-thirty in case he came in and wanted anything. I remember thinking that I'd only have about twenty-five minutes more and I was sleepy. And then pretty soon at twelve-thirty I went to bed."

"As you passed Mrs. Thane's door on your way upstairs did you notice anything peculiar?"

"No, sir." Even Emma Bloomstead's garrulity was stemmed as the thought that she had passed a room containing a murdered woman at twelve-thirty at night.

"Was the door open?"

"I didn't notice."

"You went right to bed and to sleep? You didn't hear any noise or sound in the house?"

"No, sir."

"No sound of a shot?"

"No, sir."

"When you were in your sitting room in the basement you heard nothing?"

"Oh no, you couldn't hear yourself shout with that racket going on down there where they're building the subway."

"In other words, neither before or after you went to bed did you hear the sound of a shot."

"That's right."

"And what was the next thing you knew after you had gone to sleep?"

"Well, the next thing I knew, the bell in my room was ringing and I came down here, and Mr. Thane was here and—" Emma looked apprehensively in the direction of the bedroom.

"And what did you find?"

"Mr. Thane was over there—" and she nodded toward the archway, "bending over Mrs. Thane sort of shaking her like he was trying to make her talk. He was sort of wild-like, and trembling, and talking fast. And he told me to call Dr. Partridge next door. So I tried to get the doctor, but the telephone wouldn't work, so then I went over there myself and Dr. Partridge came right over with me."

"You say the telephone wouldn't work?" the inspector broke in.

"Yes, sir."

"What telephone?"

"That one there," and she pointed to the instrument carefully masked behind a Dresden shepherdess with widespreading bouffant panniers. Beside it was a small indexed booklet containing addresses and telephone numbers.

Herschman crossed the room quickly and took down the receiver, but no answer came. Several times he clicked the hook but the instrument was dead.

"The one downstairs and the one up in Mr. Thane's room work, but not that one," the maid explained and Herschman's eyebrows went up. Suddenly he stooped over and examined the gilded cord that ran along the wall for a little way before disappearing into the box at the foot of the baseboard. The cord held tight against the plaster and woodwork by small staples appeared intact to the casual observer surveying it from a standing height. But as the inspector bent down he gave a low whistle.

"Cut!" and he indicated a point near the box where a closer scrutiny revealed the severed strands.

The four of them peered down at the baseboard and the district attorney looked inquiringly at the inspector. But Herschman, if he had any theory to offer, said nothing.

"The other phones in the house are they working?" Tracy inquired and the maid, nodded.

"Yes, we've been using them this morning. And last night I called the police on the one downstairs."

"That was after you came back here with Dr. Partridge?"

"Yes, sir. He came right up here and looked at Mrs. Thane and said she was dead and then Mr. Thane told me to call the police."

"Is Dr. Partridge available now?"

"Do you mean can you get him?"

The district attorney nodded.

"Yes, sir. He went home just a little while ago, and I guess maybe he's still there, because he don't go out much."

The district attorney made a motion of dismissal and Emma quit the room reluctantly. At the doorway she paused, hoping obviously that the keenly enjoyable situation might be prolonged by a suddenly remembered question. But none was forthcoming.

"Suppose you have one of the men outside bring the doctor over," Tracy said to the inspector. "I'd like to have a—what in the devil are *you* doing?"

Left to his own devices during the course of the questioning, Spike had been wandering about the room in an aimless contemplation of knickknacks, fiddling with the pillows of the chaise longue, gravely contemplating the ornaments of the writing desk, staring meditatively into ash trays. Now he was at the dressing table and from its litter of crystal and silver toilet articles he had chosen a lip stick and was carefully painting a simpering Cupid's bow on his own firm lips. At the sound of his brother's voice he turned a ludicrous smile upon the room.

"*What* in the devil are you doing?" The district attorney as was his habit when upset, repeated himself with growing emphasis.

"Charming, isn't it?" and Spike lighted a cigarette, just as if it were quite the thing for gentlemen at murder investigations to spend their time smearing pale orange rouge on their lips.

It was with difficulty that the district attorney controlled himself. For a moment he seemed on the verge of sputtering like an irate teakettle. Then he spoke with reproving hauteur.

"This, my dear brother, let me remind you, for you seem to have forgotten yourself, is not a vaudeville performance."

It was only the presence of the doctor and the inspector that kept him from elaborating the theme into another brother-to-brother lecture. His impulse was to repeat all the accusations of the morning with a few extra thrown in to fit the occasion. He was grateful for the arrival of Dr. Partridge, turning the attention of Herschman and the medical examiner from the humiliating sight of his own brother making a blasted fool of himself.

Peregrine. Partridge's name was his most adequate description. In christening him thus, his parents in the remote Victorian past had divined with remarkable foresight that some day their offspring would grow up to resemble nothing so much in the world as—Peregrine Partridge. A little, fussy, meticulous man with bright bird eyes and a bustling air that did not match at all the sad droop of his walrus mustache.

It was apparent from his attitude as he greeted the district attorney that he was fully aware of his own importance in the case, and like Emma was quite a little setup by it. His chest beneath his old-fashioned, double-breasted vest puffed out with a slight pompousness—but not too far out. It was more than ten years since he had been in active practice of his profession, but he had not forgotten the correct bearing in the presence of death— particularly death under, strange and mysterious circumstances.

"If you would be so kind, Dr. Partridge," said Tracy, "I wish you would repeat for me the things which you told Inspector Herschman here earlier in the morning"

The little doctor was on the verge of saying, "Delighted!" but recalled himself in time. For a moment he considered Tracy's request in grave silence. Then he began his story in a careful, precise voice.

"Mr. Thane, as you doubtless know, spent the evening with me. Or rather I should say part of the morning. We are both troubled with insomnia and frequently we keep each other company over the chessboard. Last night we played until about a quarter of four. He hadn't been gone more than five minutes when Emma, the maid, came over to my house in great agitation and asked me to come over here. I came and found Mrs. Thane—dead."

He paused to let the full drama of his recital sink in.

"Would you tell us the position in which you found the body?"

"It was lying in precisely the position it is in now. I see your man has not disturbed it in the slightest detail."

"And did you make any examination?"

"Yes, a brief, but somewhat thorough one under the circumstances."

"What in your opinion was the time at which Mrs. Thane was killed?"

"Probably around twelve o'clock. Possibly a little before, possibly a little after. But certainly not after one."

Both Herschman and Tracy looked toward the medical examiner, struck by the similarity of the two doctors' findings. Then Tracy turned back to Dr. Partridge and posed his next question with tactful caution.

"Did you by any chance, Doctor, know this Spencer who took Mrs. Thane out last night?"

"Only by hearsay. Mr. Thane sometimes spoke of him."

"He was friendly with him?"

"Well, not exactly that. Mr. Thane and the young chap were not quite of the same mental caliber, the same tastes. But Mr. Thane was tolerant toward him. He understood Mrs. Thane's desire for dancing and theaters, and as he did not care to go himself, he raised no objections. I understand—" He hesitated as if uncertain of the propriety of the statement. "I understand she paid him well."

"Oh, a professional gigolo?"

"Something of the sort."

"The Schlockenhass case again," Herschman put in and the district attorney nodded.

"The what?" the little doctor asked.

"The Schlockenhass murder about six months ago."

"Oh, yes, I recall. There was a great deal in the papers at the time."

"Tell me, Doctor," Tracy went on, "after you made your examination of Mrs. Thane and ascertained that she was dead, what did you do?"

"I turned my attention to Mr. Thane. I could see that the living had more need of my services than the dead. Mr. Thane has for several years been a victim of chronic heart disease. He was suffering from shock, natural enough under the circumstances, but with increased severity in his particular case. After the police arrived, I persuaded him to leave things in their hands and to: come over to my house with me."

"And he is there now?"

"Yes, I suppose you would like to question him?"

"Of course, but if you think he is unable just at present, we could put it off for a few hours."

"No, I think perhaps it would be best if you saw him now. I gave him a sedative but the effects are beginning to wear off. It might do him good to talk"

"Very well, then, Doctor," Tracy indicated the doorway and the four of them—the district attorney, the inspector, Dr. Partridge and Spike went down the stairs to the first floor in follow-the-leader formation. But at the foot of the stairs just as they were prepared to leave the house, Emma appeared.

"Mr. Thane's come home," she announced, "and he says that if the policemen would like to see him he's up in his rooms."

The apartment of Elton Thane was on the same plan as that of his wife and directly above it But there the similarity ended. These were a man's rooms—dull greens and browns; soft, worn leather chairs; heavy walnut furniture bearing the marks of long wear; the carpet a little threadbare; smoking stands at comfortable intervals—a room that bore the stamp of living rather than the impress of an interior decorator's latest whim.

When the four men entered the room Elton Thane was standing looking out of the front windows, his back to the door. He was a tall man with bushy, iron-gray hair, and shoulders that drooped as if suddenly he had been dealt a staggering blow in the back. At the sound of their entrance, he turned slowly.

In his youth he had undoubtedly been a handsome man. Now at fifty he was still strikingly good looking, but time had bracketed his mouth with two heavy lines, and dulled the deep-set brown eyes. He was haggard, and his clothes were crumpled by the restless sleep from which he had just awakened. His face as he stood before them was curiously devoid of expression as if the tragedy of the night had left him stunned and but partly conscious of what was going on around him.

For a moment he only stood there, slowly taking in the presence of the four men. Then he motioned them to chairs and seated himself.

"Well?" A single syllable, but it was as if his voice had stuck in a parched throat.

"Mr. Thane," the district attorney began, "this is a very painful procedure for you, and I regret sincerely that it is necessary. However, you understand—"

Thane nodded silently, and Tracy continued. "Will you please tell us in as much detail as possible everything you know of the movement of Mrs. Thane last night."

There was a slight pause. Then in a low, controlled voice Elton Thane spoke. His story was substantially that of the maid and Dr. Partridge. After his wife had left at eight o'clock, he had written a letter, sent the maid out to post it, and had then gone off to his club, the Chatham, on West Seventy-sixth Street.

At some time about twelve he had returned to Eighty-second Street to Dr. Partridge's and played chess until about four in the morning, and had then gone home. Passing his wife's door and noticing the light, he had knocked. When there was no answer he had gone in and found her dead body lying in front of the rifled safe.

He paused, but his face, still as expressionless as ever, remained set.

"Tell me, Mr. Thane," said the district attorney, tactfully switching the conversation from this painful situation, "what do you know about this young fellow, Spencer?"

For a moment Elton Thane hesitated. "Well," he said finally, "I really know very little about him. He was— ah—"

"I think I understand. He was your wife's paid companion on dining and dancing excurions which you yourself did not care to attend." Thane nodded.

"Anything more than that?"

"No!" For the first time he raised his voice and his eyes flashed. Then as if this effort had suddenly weakened him he slumped into his chair and his hands hung limp over the upholstered arms. When he spoke again he had regained his control. "No, I am quite sure that there was nothing more between them than that. My wife was a good deal younger than I and—our tastes were different."

"Was he here frequently?"

"Twice each week. He was always engaged for Monday and Thursday evenings."

"And you were friendly with him?"

Thane nodded. "He was—he—I liked him. He seemed a good sort. As a matter of fact I took him golfing with me several times. I can't believe that—that—"

"That he is the murderer of your wife."

As his unspoken thoughts were put into words by the district attorney, Elton Thane gripped the arms of his chair until his knuckles showed white. But he only repeated himself.

"I can't believe it."

"Were there any other people in the house last night between eight and twelve?"

"No one, except the maid and myself and Spencer."

"Who beside Mrs. Thane knew the combination to the safe in her bedroom?"

"I was the only other person."

"Do you, by any chance, know where Spencer lives?"

"He used to have an apartment somewhere on West One Hundred and Fourth Street, between Columbus Avenue and the Park. I don't know the exact number, but I was there two or three times after we had played golf together. He has moved recently though. I think it's some place not far from here but I can't say just where."

"Perhaps," said the district attorney turning to Herschman, "you might find the telephone number on the pad in Mrs. Thane's room"

"As if I hadn't already thought of that," the inspector replied "The S page is missing. The only page in the alphabet that isn't there"

III. The Little Round Hole in the Chaise Longue

AS Tracy, Herschman and Spike drove back to Police Headquarters, the two older men reviewed briefly the famous Schlockenhass case which had stirred the city six months before.

Greta Schlockenhass, middle-aged wife of a rich brewer, owner of many gaudy but expensive jewels had been found dead in her hotel apartment, a bullet through her heart and $150,000 worth of jewels missing. Investigation showed that she had been seen frequently in the company of several sleek young men in the night clubs. For their service as escorts she had paid them generously. Four of them were taken into custody by the police, but there had never been sufficient evidence to charge them with the crime, although two of them already had records for larceny. They had been released. The murderer had never been found nor, the jewels recovered.

The story had been a newspaper sensation for four weeks, with flaunting eight-column streamer heads, pictures of the murdered woman, her bereaved but complacent husband and the four young gigolos who had had the misfortune to be in her employ.

"Suppose we have a look at the Schlockenhass records when we get back to the office," the district attorney suggested.

"I was thinking the same thing myself," Herschman replied "Milliken should be ready with the fingerprints by then."

"In the meantime," Spike suggested, entering the conversation for the first time since his rebuff over the rouge incident, "let's read all about it in the newspapers."

The taxi held up by traffic was stopped immediately in front of a newsstand which had just received its pile of first editions of the afternoon papers. Spike beckoned to the boy in charge.

"A *Sun* and an *Evening Post* for these two," he said, "and a nice, juicy *Graphic* for me"

The taxi moved on and the three of them leaned back in contemplation of their papers—the district attorney with a certain distasteful apprehension—the inspector with an air of abstraction as if he were thinking of other things.

But Spike rustled his with gusto. "As usual," he said after a glance at the front page, "my trusty tab's about six hours ahead of yours. Here's the whole story."

And there indeed it was. Ninety-six-point headlines. "Diamond Queen Slain." Photographs of Cecily Thane and her husband resurrected from the office morgue. The Thane house decorated with an ominous X. "Police Seek Night-Club Sheik." Emma Bloomstead showing rather too much leg.

The district attorney gave one brief, pained glance at the gaudy page and heaved a sigh of resignation.

"It's begun," he said.

And when he reached the anteroom of his office at Headquarters, the full tide of it swept over him. The room was full of newspaper men, and rather irate newspaper men at that. Each one of them had received a thorough reprimand from the city desk for the manner in which the *Graphic* had beat them on the first-edition story. It was the only paper in town that carried the news.

It was twenty minutes before the inspector and the district attorney could escape the mob and their questions, but finally they emerged into the district attorney's private office where Spike had already made himself comfortable.

Milliken, fingerprint expert, had been even quicker in his work than the inspector had anticipated, and had already a group of photographs to lay before his chief. Both Tracy and Herschman were struck with the same thought as they looked at them—the records in the Schlockenhass case—and Lovelace, Tracy's secretary, was accordingly sent after them.

"A nice variety," Milliken explained as he laid the still damp prints on the desk. "At least four different persons."

Tracy and Herschman examined the pictures with interest. Each one was neatly labeled with the exact spot in the room from which it was taken . . . from the edge of the mantelpiece . . . a corner of the dressing table . . . the arm of a chair.

"Anything on the wall safe?" the inspector inquired.

"Couldn't get a trace. It had apparently been wiped clean."

"Hm." The inspector appeared to consider this piece of information, but the arrival of Lovelace with the Schlockenhass records interrupted whatever train of thought it might have aroused.

There were a number of legal papers and two photographs, one front and one profile view of each of the four men who had been arrested in the famous jewel-murder of the year before. And underneath each photograph were five neat fingerprints.

It was with these prints that Milliken at the inspector's direction quickly compared the prints which had been taken from the room of Cecily Thane that morning. He had been at work with his small pocket glass no more than three minutes when he looked up with an expression of satisfaction, and pushed two of the pictures toward the two men eagerly waiting on the other side of the table.

"There's your man," he said quietly. And then with a tiny steel rod he proceeded to point out the similarity in markings. The thumb and forefinger print which had been taken from the edge of a small smoking table in

Cecily Thane's bedroom was identical with the corresponding prints of one of the Schlockenhass arrests.

Herschman read from the back of the record card: "William Preston . . . 23 years old . . . 5 ft. 8 . . . weight 140 pounds . . . brown eyes . . . occupation professional dancer. No criminal record. . . . Was seen at the Lido Venice with Greta Schlockenhass three hours before her murdered body was discovered."

"Well," said the inspector, "it looks like the man we're after is the right one. Must have changed his name to Spencer."

A wave of obvious relief seemed to sweep over the district attorney at this satisfactory turn of the case. For the first time that morning he leaned back in his chair and relaxed, and the worried frown faded from between his brows.

The striking coincidence of the murder of Greta Schlockenhass and Cecily Thane under the same circumstances and with, obviously enough, at least one person involved in both cases, seemed to clear the way for a solution of the puzzle.

When Herschman and Milliken had left, Tracy helped himself to a cigar, lighted it in a leisurely fashion and looked in the direction of his brother. Spike, as was his habit, had immediately upon entering the room selected the most comfortable chair and slouched into it. While his brother, the inspector and the fingerprint expert had made their comparison of the fingerprints, he had been gazing out of the window at the gloomy, barred windows of the Tombs just across the street.

"Well," said Tracy complacently, "you see how it's done."

"How what's done?" Spike asked, pulling his mind back apparently from a long distance.

"You wanted to see how criminals are found out," he explained patiently, "and now you see it. Not so thrilling after all, is it?"

"In other words, you mean that this chap Spencer popped off Mrs. Thane?"

"Exactly."

Spike reached forth a hand and picked up the four sets of pictures from the Schlockenhass case and examined them one by one. Three of them were sleek-looking young fellows with carefully brilliantined hair, the type that can be seen by the dozens on any dance floor. But the fourth one, marked Preston, was different. The hair was an unruly dark mop. And the eyes were not the knowing eyes of a professional dancing man, but of a boy who seemed to have stumbled somehow into trouble. The chin both in profile and full face was weak, but the general effect of the face as a whole was somewhat appealing.

Spike looked at the picture carefully for a few moments. "Aren't you jumping at conclusions?" he said.

Tracy laughed indulgently. "The amateur detective has a theory?"

"Not a theory. Just a couple of questions."

"Let me have them and perhaps I can clear it up for you." Tracy was patronizing.

"Well, number one is, why, if this Spencer lad did do the trick, why did he take the trouble to lug the body from the chaise longue to the spot in front of the safe? Why not just leave the lady where she lay?"

"What do you mean?"

"I mean that she wasn't killed in front of the safe. Number two—why—"

"My dear fellow, I never heard anything so ridiculous."

"Quit 'my dear fellowing' me and hear me the to end. We are alone. No outsiders are present to witness the humiliating depth of my foolishness in thinking I can put my feeble brain against the mighty minds of the legal and police departments, so let me babble on.

"As I said before—number two—who was the woman, beside Emma, of course, who was in Cecily Thane's sitting room between eight o'clock last night and four this morning?"

"Now you're talking like one of your infernal tabloids. I wish you would read the *Times* occasionally and then your mind would not run so constantly to women."

"Just the same," Spike persisted, "it would be interesting to know"

From his inside pocket he drew out his cigarette case and opened it. But he did not take out a cigarette, for there were no fresh ones in it—only five half-smoked butts.

"You were justified, my dear brother," he said, "in thinking I was an utter damn fool this morning, playing with the late Mrs. Thane's lip stick. But as a matter of fact it was one of my infrequent sensible moments."

For a few seconds he held the open cigarette case before him and contemplated the five butts. Then one by one he lifted them out and put them on the desk before him.

"These two Luckies I found in the ash tray immediately to the right of the big easy-chair by the fireplace. You'll note that they're ringed with dark carmine rouge, the kind usually affected by dashing brunettes. And these two Benson and Hedges I found in the ash tray beside the chaise longue. They are, please observe, ringed with a much lighter shade of roug—pale orange in fact. And this Camel I smoked myself after I had painted the engaging Cupid's bow. The color on it corresponds exactly with that on the Benson and Hedges. And the maid said that she emptied the ash trays at eight o'clock after Mrs. Thane had gone out."

He paused to let these carefully assorted facts sink in.

"Which means?" said the district attorney

"Which means that when Mrs. Thane came home last night she smoked two cigarettes. And that some other woman was also in the room some time after eight o'clock when the maid emptied the ash trays and she too smoked two cigarettes. Under the circumstances, I think it would be rather interesting to know just who she was."

For a moment the district attorney said nothing, but shifted uneasily. "But did it occur to you," he said finally, "that the dark red lip rouge might belong also to Mrs. Thane?"

"Nothing, my dear brother, escapes me. I made a special point of taking an inventory of all Mrs. Thane's lip sticks on the dresser and in the drawers and all were the same shade—pale orange."

"Probably the maid sat down and took a rest while she was clearing things up."

"Probably," Spike shrugged his shoulders as if to let the subject drop.

"Means nothing," Tracy went on. It was plain that he was trying to lull his reason to sleep and let these disquieting points brought up by his brother rest unnoticed. "Herschman will probably be able to find a perfectly logical explanation in five minutes."

"Probably," Spike admitted. Then he reached for a cigarette from a paper packet in the pocket of his Tuxedo: and lit it and exhaled deeply.

"I wonder," he said, "I wonder if her eyes are blue. All my life I've been searching for a blue-eyed brunette and the only one I ever saw was a Dublin barmaid who had a husband who was forty pounds heavier than I. A charming little thing but really not—"

"Look here, Philip, the district attorney broke in, "you are an utter damn fool, but—but—"

"But sometimes out of the mouths of babes, sucklings and damn fools there sprout words of wisdom."

Tracy nodded grudgingly. "This cigarette business does look slightly suspicious. But on what do you base your statement that the body was moved from the chaise longue to the position in which it was discovered in front of the safe."

"I'm not so sure about that," Spike admitted. "I just threw that in by way of rousing your appetite for more and bloodier details. Still, I think I'm right at that."

Suddenly he rose from his chair and reached for his hat. Then he paused and looked at his brother with a certain eagerness in his glance.

"Listen, old thing, would you mind tremendously if I temporarily stepped out of my role of unofficial observer?"

"Why?"

"I'd like awfully to have another chat with the charming and gabby Emma. Not that I have ever been partial to blondes, but—"

"Certainly not. You are not going to turn this case into one of your notorious escapades with women, and a servant girl at that."

"My dear Richard, you wrong me. My pursuit of Emma is purely in the interests of criminal investigation. I shall do and say nothing in her presence that you and dear old Great-grandmother Tracy couldn't witness and retain your innocency. What I mean to suggest is not a rendezvous tête-a-tête, but a serious little chat. Just you and me and Emma. Something clubby—and revealing."

For a moment the district attorney hesitated.

"Very well," he said. "It isn't at all regular, but—" and he too reached for his hat.

"Oh, by the way," Spike said as he paused at the door, "would you mind bringing the fatal bullet along with you?"

In a few moments they were in a taxi speeding north for the second time that morning to Eighty-second Street.

"Another thing that's funny," Spike pointed out, "is that cut telephone wire."

"A very common precaution," the district attorney assured him.

"But in this case why was it necessary. Granting that this fellow Spencer did do the dirty deed, certainly he gave the lady no time to summon help before he shot her. And she was hardly in any condition to do it afterward."

The district attorney, if he had an explanation, did not offer it, and Spike continued more in the manner of one thinking aloud than conversing.

"The fingerprint business on the safe is intriguing too. If Spencer is the guilty guy he probably waited until she went to the safe of her own accord to put something away or take something out. And then he plugged her. But why wipe off her fingerprints?" He broke off, bewildered by the maze of his speculations.

As they stopped before the Thane house, the police ambulance carrying its grisly burden was backing away from the door. Cecily Thane's bedroom was just as they had left it, except for the spot immediately in front of the safe. An ugly dark stain spread out through the carpet where the body had lain. Two policemen were standing guard, one inside the two-room apartment and one in the hall outside. Tracy requested one of them to summon the maid.

As Emma entered the room a few moments later both the district attorney and Spike were struck by the change in her attitude. Her self-assurance was gone and she seemed noticeably more subdued than she had been in the morning. It was plain that this second interview filled her with no elating sense of importance. She eyed the two men with a certain uneasy distrust and said nothing.

Spike glanced questioningly at his brother, and the district attorney nodded to him. "Go ahead —but—" He broke off with a warning, apprehensive, look as if to say, "Go ahead, but try not to make *too* much of a fool of yourself."

Spike courteously indicated a chair, and Emma, unused to such mannerly treatment by the strange invaders who had been swarming the house since four o'clock that morning, seated herself uneasily on the edge. He opened his cigarette case, now replenished and offered her one fraternally. The district attorney frowned.

"Smoke?"

She shook her head. "No, sir."

"Never?"

"No, sir."

He selected one for himself and lit it and settled back comfortably in his chair.

"You really should learn to smoke, my girl," he advised sagely. "Splendid for the nerves."

"Yes, sir. That's what Mrs. Thane always said."

"And Mrs. Thane was very nervous?"

"Well—yes—lately."

"You've known Mrs. Thane a long time, haven't you?"

"I've worked here five years."

"Then you're pretty well acquainted with all of her friends, aren't you?"

"Yes, sir."

A sudden change seemed to come over Spike. He sobered, left off his casual air, like one who has dallied long enough and has decided to come down to business. As he posed the next question there was nothing in his manner to indicate that he had but a few hours before placed elk-hunting and criminal investigation in the same category.

He was in deadly earnest, and Emma grew more uneasy under his direct gaze.

"Tell me," he said, "did any of Mrs. Thane's friends drop in to call last night after she left with Mr. Spencer?"

"Why—no."

"No—women friends, for instance?"

"No, sir."

"Did she have any visitors earlier in the evening before she left?"

"Well—about six o'clock her brother came to see her."

"Her brother?"

"Yes, Mr. George Griffis."

"He is a frequent caller, I suppose?"

"No, he doesn't come very often—not since he moved away."

"He used to live here?"

"Yes, sir, until about a year ago."

"And this is the first time he has been in the house in a year?"

"Yes, sir."

"Sort of a family reunion?"

"Well—not exactly."

"What do you mean—not exactly?"

"I mean that—that—" She broke off abruptly with a look almost of fright in her eyes. "You'd —you'd better ask Mr. Thane."

"I see." Spike paused a moment. Then he continued his questions.

"Did Mrs. Thane go out at any time during the day?"

"No, sir, she was in all day."

"Did she have any other visitors except Mr. Spencer and her brother?"

Emma hesitated and ran her tongue over dry lips before she answered. "No, sir."

"Did she write any letters?"

"I don't know."

"What I mean is did she send you out with any to post?"

"No, sir."

"Perhaps she had you call a messenger?"

"Yes, sir."

"Did she send many letters that way—by messenger?"

"Well—quite a few—lately."

"You don't know by any chance to whom the one she sent yesterday was directed?"

"No, sir."

"But you called the messenger for her?"

Emma nodded.

"Western Union?"

"No, sir. Service."

Spike took a long pull at his cigarette before he spoke again. Then: "You are quite sure—quite sure, mind you—that no one came to the house after Mrs. Thane left last night?"

"Why—no sir." The denial was emphatic, but even as she made it, her feet shifted nervously.

He considered this for a moment. Then abruptly he changed his tack.

"Have you any idea when the furniture in this room was bought?"

The girl looked at him in slight bewilderment, unable to grasp the connection between the furniture and the murder of her late mistress, but a look of relief came over her at the sudden turn in the questioning.

"Well, Mrs. Thane was always buying new things and throwing away the old ones."

"Did she buy anything new recently?"

"She had the rooms done over about two months ago and she got that writing table and the radio cabinet and that chaise longue and the new easy-chair here."

"You did the dusting in here"

She nodded.

"When is the last time you remember dusting thoroughly?"

"Yesterday morning"

"And I suppose that in the course of your work you dusted that piece over there?" He indicated the chaise longue, soft maple wood and fine wicker skillfully combined.

"Yes, sir."

"You took all the pillows off?"

"Yes, sir."

"And you noticed nothing strange about it?"

"No, sir."

Spike rose and crossed the room to the chaise longue and swept aside its burden of down pillows.

"You didn't by any chance notice this hole, did you?"

The eyes of both the district attorney and the maid widened as they followed the direction of his finger. Through the fine wickerwork of the back, about the spot which normally supports the shoulder blade, was a small, round hole, with still fresh edges of wicker showing.

"I think, Richard," said Spike on whom the old air of nonchalance had suddenly descended "I think you'll find that the bullet which your man picked up back there in the bedroom just fit this hole."

IV. Blots on a Blotter

FOR a few moments after the maid had left the room, Tracy stood gaping at the hole in the chaise longue. Then slowly he drew a small bit of lead from his pocket and passed it through the opening. Even as Spike had predicted, it fitted exactly. Quickly he turned to his brother in agitation.

"I can hardly see how even that alters the case," he protested in feeble defense. "He might just as easily have killed her here as over there."

"Of course, but what would be his object in lugging the body across the room and depositing it melodramatically amid the empty jewel cases unless—"

Spike stopped abruptly as if he had suddenly chanced on an idea.

"Unless what?"

"Unless the person who did it was aiming for just that. A woman shot through the heart . . . safe empty . . . the jewels gone. Plain as day. Motive robbery."

"I don't follow you."

"Of course, old dear. Don't try, you'll strain your brain attempting to keep up with my light fling deductions. You really should read the tabs, though, and you would be able to dope these things out better."

"But the dent which the bullet made in the woodwork over there is as plain as day."

"Certainly. You or I or any one else could duplicate it in two minutes with a nail and a shoe to pound it in."

"And your theory about a third person—possibly a woman—having been here is totally erroneous."

"Oh, do you think so?"

"Didn't the maid deny that any one else had been in the house?"

"Certainly, but she was lying. Did you notice that she didn't say 'No' right out when I asked her. She said, 'Why—no'. I always suspect denial when it's prefaced by 'Why.' I'm rather struck, too, by the change in Emma. I'm afraid she's losing her grip."

"Yes," Tracy admitted, "she doesn't seem to be so—so self-assured as she was this morning."

"I rather imagine she's been talking to some one since we were here this morning, and she has been warned against too much gab."

"Thane, perhaps."

"I shouldn't be surprised. Let's have another talk with him."

Tracy nodded assent and rose to summon the officer just outside the door, but Spike stopped him.

"Just a moment. This messenger business intrigues me frightfully. Suppose we find out first just where Mrs. Thane's letter was sent yesterday afternoon."

In a few moments he had the Service Messenger Company on the telephone in the lower front hall. At first they were unwilling to give out the information, but the name of the district attorney of New York County soon brought a more satisfactory answer.

"Our messenger called at the Thane house about four yesterday afternoon and took a letter to Mrs. Mortimer Fennel at 204 West Eighty-sixth Street," the voice over the wire admitted.

"Was there any answer?"

Spike hung up the receiver and took the stairs to the second floor two at a time. As he entered the sitting room his eyes traveled with a speculative glint to the writing table on the opposite side of the room. From the dressing table in the bedroom he brought a hand glass.

"Blotters," he explained to his brother, "are always interesting. Especially the blotters of ladies who have just been murdered. Or, at least, that is the way it has been in all the detective stories I've ever read."

The writing pad of the desk was clear of any blots of ink, but the small hand blotter, mounted on a pale blue and green enameled pad, bore several marks. It was apparently a fresh one, for what impressions there were stood out clearly, and only in one or two places were there marks superimposed upon others.

Spike held the looking-glass at right angles and the two men examined the reflection.

"Frightfully disappointing, isn't it," Spike admitted "I was all prepared for blackmail, rape, arson and blood. Still, we'll keep it for future reference," and he extracted the blotter from its holder and handed it over to his brother. "And now let's get at Thane."

Elton Thane was still in his apartment on the third floor, but when he was informed by one of the ubiquitous officers that the district attorney wished to speak to him again, he came down to the reception room on the first floor and waited for him there. By tacit agreement it was Tracy who posed the questions this time. Although willing to trust his brother in conversation with inconsequential servant girls, he was not willing to grant him an equal privilege with the master of the house.

"I'm sorry to disturb you again, Mr. Thane," he explained, "but there are a few points which are not yet quite clear to me. My brother here is—ah—assisting in the investigation so you need not feel constrained by his presence," he added as he noted Thane eyeing Spike skeptically.

"We understand that your wife had some visitors yesterday."

For a moment Elton Thane said nothing, merely looked out of the window, his lower lip caught between his teeth. Then with his eyes still averted he spoke.

"Yes?" but the word was a question rather than a confirmation.

"Yes. The maid tells us that Mrs. Thane's brother was here yesterday afternoon."

"Yes, he was," he admitted quietly.

"And what was his mission?"

"I don't know. I wasn't here at the time."

"But surely your wife told you."

"No, I came in at six and she was resting. I did not disturb her. I did not see her until just before she left and Spencer was with her. All she said was, 'George was here this afternoon.'"

"This is his first visit for quite a while, isn't it?"

"Yes. In almost a year. He used to live here with us."

"And why did he leave?"

"He preferred living closer to his place of business. He has a small real estate business in Nassau Street, and he found it more convenient to live on Brooklyn Heights."

"You have his address?"

"Only his office. 154 Nassau Street."

"There were no—no hard feelings when he left?"

"None whatever. As a matter of fact he still keeps his room here, in a way."

"What do you mean, 'in a way'?"

"I mean he still kept his latchkey, and his bedroom on the first floor has remained the same since he left it. He was free at any time to come and go in the house as he pleased."

"And did he ever avail himself of that privilege?"

Thane paused to think. "As a matter of fact, I don't believe he ever did."

"So that yesterday, to the best of your knowledge, is the first time that he has been in this house for a year?"

"Yes."

There was a short pause while the district attorney considered these statements. Then he switched to a new tack.

"And did your wife have any other visitors that you know of yesterday?"

"No women visitors, for instance?"

"No."

"No one by any chance came to the house to see her after she had gone out with Spencer."

"Why—no."

Again a short pause. Spike's glance met his brother's in silent appeal. The district attorney hesitated uncertainly and then nodded almost imperceptibly.

"My dear Mr. Thane," said Spike in a leisurely tone which was in pleasing contrast to the hammer-like quality of his brother's questioning, "would you mind my offering a bit of advice?"

"Why no."

"I mean that if you really intend to be convincingly you should leave off the 'Why'."

Elton Thane stiffened, and a slow red crept up his pale ears.

"What do you mean?"

"I mean just this—we have a very strong suspicion that some one beside Spencer and Mrs. Thane's brother came to this house last night."

"Why, I never heard of anything so preposterous."

"Really, Mr. Thane, it will be much simpler if you just tell us right off the bat. Certain things make me feel that it was a woman."

"A woman?"

"Oh, so it wasn't a woman. Well then, a man."

For a moment Elton Thane remained stiff and erect in his chair. Then suddenly he seemed to give way to the inevitable. He slumped back with a gesture of surrender.

"All right," he said, "I'll admit it. But—but may I ask you, if you possibly can, not to drag this man into the case?" There was a note almost of anguish in his voice

"You may rest assured," the district attorney broke in, "that we shall do everything we can to avoid involving innocent persons. But under the circumstances, we cannot know who is innocent and who is suspect, unless you are perfectly frank with us."

Thane nodded in assent. "You're quite right. Forgive me for my efforts to conceal—"

"And who was this man?"

"He was a very old friend of both Mrs. Thane and myself. He and his wife and daughter used to live in the same apartment house with us before we moved here. We have known them for perhaps twelve or fifteen years. He came to the house last night after both of us had left. Emma tells me that he said that he would come in and wait a while, thinking I might possibly return from the club. He went up to Mrs. Thane's sitting room—that's where we usually met—and stayed for a little while and then left."

"And was he alone?"

"Yes."

"He had no—no woman friend with him?"

"He was quite alone. His wife is an invalid—has been for many years. And as a matter of fact she has recently taken a turn for the worse. That is the main reason why I hope that his name can be kept out of it, even in the most innocuous connection. She is a very highly strung woman, and if she should hear about it in any way, it might have an extremely bad effect on her at this particular time."

"I quite understand. And what is this man's name?"

"Mortimer Fennel."

V. THE ROUGE-RINGED CIGARETTE

THE district attorney and his brother walked briskly along Eighty-sixth Street in the direction of Riverside Drive and exchanged arguments.

"But my dear fellow," Tracy protested, "surely Thane told a straight enough story—after we pressed him—"

"After 'we' pressed him?" Spike laughed. "Straight enough for you, but not for me."

"Well, what lurid idea have you got up your sleeve now?"

"It's so lurid that even I blush to confess it."

"What is it?"

"Well, when a lady writes a note to a gentleman's wife and that very same night the gentleman comes to the lady's house and subsequently the lady is found dead with a bullet through her heart—well, it all sounds rather intriguing, don't you think?"

"Possibly, if I could follow you."

"The thing that puzzles me though is where my blue-eyed brunette—at least I hope she's a blue-eyed brunette—with the heavy, carmine lipstick comes in. I hesitate to accuse Mr. Fennel, sight unseen, of using rouge."

"And I hope that I can trust you to refrain from even making any ridiculous suggestion in that direction."

"Oh, positively. I shall be as silent as the tomb—unless, of course, you get in a corner as you did with Thane, just now." He grinned out of the side of his eyes at his brother.

"You know," he went on, "I can't get over the change in Emma. She was positively clam-like in comparison with her garrulous state this morning."

"Probably a let-down after the initial excitement of the case. It frequently affects people that way."

"Richard, dear, your psychology is rotten—and frightfully unexciting. I prefer to think that some one has forcibly impressed upon her the golden quality of silence. As my feeble brain has it figured out, Thane had no opportunity to talk to her until after we left this morning. And when he did he found out that this George Griffis and Mortimer Fennel had visited the house the night before. And for some reason which as yet I can't quite fathom, he would much rather these two gentlemen were left out of the case. This Mortimer Fennel especially."

The district attorney only grunted and the two of them walked on in silence—Tracy in heavy gloom; Spike with a singularly exhilarated air about him.

Number 204 West Eighty-sixth Street was a six-story apartment house of the older type distinguished by an oversupply of baroque ornament and a lobby that had originally been marble and red plush. Now all that remained of former glories were yellowed stone and worn armchairs, and an iron-grilled elevator presided over by an ancient black man. Its proximity to Riverside Drive gave it a certain air of refinement, while its out-of-date design stamped it as a place for people of limited means.

The Fennel apartment was on the sixth floor. As the district attorney and his brother stood in the hall outside the door waiting for an answer to their ring, Spike pulled out his watch.

"Twelve o'clock. We're just in time for lunch."

"I hardly think you have the proper costume for a luncheon engagement," Tracy remind him with a disapproving glance. Spike was still wearing the crumpled Tuxedo which he had slept in at the Forty-seventh Precinct Station House.

"Oh, that's not what's bothering me," he assured his brother. "I was just wondering whether by any chance Mr. Fennel has read of the recent disturbance on Eighty-second Street. I don't imagine he reads the *Graphic* and the other papers wouldn't have it until their second edition. If not, we—"

His sentence was cut short by the opening of the door. It gave on to one of those long dark halls for which the older New York apartments are famous, so that it was difficult at first for them to make out the figure of the girl who answered their ring.

"Mr. Mortimer Fennel?" the district attorney inquired.

"You wished to see him?"

"Yes."

"Won't you come in," and she led the way down the dark hall to the living room in the front. It was a comfortable looking place, tasteful and pleasant with gay chintz hangings and the soft gleam of old walnut and polished brass andirons. The girl motioned them to sit down, but she did not immediately summon Mortimer Fennel.

She was a young woman of perhaps twenty-two or three but her somewhat Junoesque build made her seem older. Almost as tall as Spike, she was handsome rather than pretty. There was a certain firm line to her chin that gave one the feeling that in character as well as figure she was a person of exceptional strength.

"Mortimer Fennel is my father," she explained. "Is there anything that I could do?"

"I'm afraid not, Miss Fennel," the district attorney said.

"You see, my mother is very ill, and my father is with her. He doesn't like to leave her even for a moment, unless it is very important."

"I'm very sorry to trouble him, but it is important."

"Very well," and she left the room with that soft tread that a sick room in the house develops.

In a few moments she returned, followed by her father. Mortimer Fennel was a man of perhaps forty-five or fifty—a strikingly handsome man. His heavy black hair, only just beginning to show gray, swept off his forehead in a Byronic gesture, and his nose, thin and sensitive, was high-arched and patrician It was his mouth that betrayed him It was full and sensual, but with a weak, defeated droop to it.

The sick vigil at his wife's bedside had told heavily on him. His unshaved face was pallid and his eyes stared out from deep circles of weariness. He had on a dressing gown over his clothes, and his shirt was collarless. For a moment he stared in slight bewilderment at the two visitors. Then the district attorney explained.

"I am exceedingly sorry to trouble you, Mr. Fennel, at this particular time, but unfortunately circumstances force me to. I am the district attorney of New York County and this is my brother who is—ah—assisting me."

As the three men seated themselves, Tracy looked inquiringly in the direction of the girl who still remained in the room.

"I would suggest that Miss Fen—"

But he was interrupted by a swift and courtly gesture from his brother. Spike drew forward a chair from one corner of the room and in his best Continental drawing-room manner bowed the girl into it. For an instant there was a lightning-like exchange of glances between the two brothers. Then Tracy capitulated.

"It has been my painful duty this morning," he went on "to investigate the murder of Cecily Thane."

Even R. Montgomery Tracy, the most unimaginative man who ever held the post of district attorney, was conscious of the crucial drama of the occasion, and had the good sense to let this single sentence stand unqualified. For a moment there was a dead silence in the room. The weak, handsome face of Mortimer Fennel suddenly, almost invisibly stiffened, but not a muscle moved. When presently he spoke, his voice seemed consciously under control.

"You mean that Mrs. Thane has been—murdered?"

Tracy nodded. "She was found at four o'clock this morning shot through the heart in the bedroom of her home."

Fennel made no move, but sat staring ahead of him. Tracy continued.

"In view of the fact that you were a visitor at the Thane house last night, Mr. Fennel, I am forced to draw you into the investigation."

"Why—why yes, certainly."

"Would you mind telling me of your visit?"

"Well—" Fennel paused to pass a thick, nervous tongue over his dry lips. "Why, I went there some time in the evening—no one was in so—so I just stayed around a bit, and then I came home."

"I'm afraid I will have to insist on a little bit more detail than that. What time, for instance was it when you went there?"'

"I—I don't remember exactly. Some time the middle of the evening. Nine o'clock perhaps."

"And who admitted you at the door?"

"Emma."

"And she told you that Mr. and Mrs. Thane were out?"

"Yes."

"But you remained for a short time?"

"Yes."

"And what did you do while you were there?"

"I—I went up to Mrs. Thane's sitting room."

"And about how long were you there?"

"Twenty minutes—perhaps half an hour."

"And what was the purpose of your visit?"

Again Fennel paused and with the same quick, nervous gesture moistened his dry lips. "Why—I was just walking by and I—I thought I would drop in for a little chat."

"Just a friendly visit?"

"Yes."

"It did not, of course, have anything to do with a letter which Mrs. Thane wrote to your wife yesterday afternoon and sent around by special messenger?"

"Well—as a matter of fact," he admitted, "it did. You see, my wife has been ill for a long time—many years.

Lately she has grown worse and—Mrs. Thane wrote just a friendly letter to cheer up a rather dismal sick room, and I thought it only courteous that I drop around and let them know of Mrs. Fennel's condition."

"You don't by any chance have the letter still?"

"I—I don't think so. I threw it in the waste basket."

"Perhaps it is still in the house?"

"No." It was the voice of Nina Fennel, sharp and decisive. "I emptied all the baskets myself this morning and it was carried away in the weekly trash removal."

Both Spike and his brother turned and looked quickly in her direction and both were struck by the contrast between the father and the daughter. He was weak, nervous, obviously uneasy. But she sat calmly in her, chair, her mouth set in a firm line and her eyes meeting those of the two men with an unwavering gaze

"Tell me, Mr. Fennel," the district attorney went on, "did you, while you were in the Thane house, see any one beside the maid?"

"No."

"As I understand it then, you went immediately to Mrs. Thane's sitting room on entering the house, remained for twenty minutes or half an hour, and then left?"

"Yes."

"And then what did you do?"

"Why—why, I came home, here"

The district attorney was silent for a moment, apparently digesting these facts and considering his next question. It was Fennel himself who broke the pause.

"Tell me—tell me more about the—murder. Who—"

"As yet there is very little to tell. We have only just begun our investigation. You don't happen to know a young chap named Spencer?"

"Spencer?"

"Tommy Spencer."

"Yes, Ce— Mrs. Thane, I believe, went about some with him."

"You knew him?"

"I've—met him."

"He is the last person whom we know to have been with Mrs. Thane."

"You mean he—killed her?"

"The investigation, as I have already pointed out, has only just begun. We have come to no conclusions as yet. You don't know where this Spencer fellow lives?"

In the questions which followed the district attorney obtained from Fennel much the same information as he had had from Thane earlier in the morning. It had been in that very apartment house that the Thanes had lived before their increased prosperity had made possible a change to a more affluent home five years before. For ten years previous to that, they had lived on the floor below, so that altogether the two families had known each other for fifteen years. But despite this long acquaintanceship, Mortimer Fennel could throw singularly little light on Cecily Thane.

"You see," he explained apologetically, "the difference in our financial status has rather come between us and the Thanes these last few years."

On the corner of Eighty-sixth Street and Riverside Drive the district attorney and his brother waited for a taxi.

"Well," said Spike, "what do you think of it all?"

"Frankly, I don't know."

"You know, old thing, you really should have paid more attention to the lady."

"Speaking of the lady, your action in keeping her in the room was quite inexcusable. Women, in so far as possible, should be kept out of police investigations."

"But my dear brother, she wasn't an ordinary woman. If you weren't quite such a doddering old bird, insensible to the charms of womankind, you would realize that Miss Nina Fennel in spite of her somewhat Amazonian proportions is an extremely likely looking gal. And—"

"That hardly qualifies her to participate in the investigation."

"—and she has black hair and the most beautiful blue eyes in the world. Furthermore, if you hadn't been wasting your glances on pa, you would have observed that when you rang in that question about the special messenger letter, the daughter attempted to quiet her jangled nerves with a cigarette."

The sarcastic reply which was on the district attorney's lips was cut short by a taxi which slid to the curb in front of them. He stepped in and waited for his brother to follow. But Spike closed the door and leaned through the window.

"If you don't mind, I think I'll take a walk along the Drive and clear the crime from my brain."

"An excellent idea," the district attorney agreed, secretly glad to be quit of his brother and his disquieting discoveries.

"But before I leave you," Spike went on, "there is one more little piece of evidence that I should surrender. Here—"

From an inside pocket he drew forth a cigarette which apparently had lived a short life. Not more than a quarter of an inch had been smoked away. And about the other end there was a circle, of deep carmine rouge.

"This," said Spike, "dropped unheeded upon the carpet from the nerveless fingers of Miss Nina Fennel when you mentioned the name of Tommy Spencer."

VI. Spike Acts Like a Low, Sneaking Cad

AT eleven o'clock of the second morning after the murder of Cecily Thane, R. Montgomery Tracy and Inspector Herschman sat in Tracy's office and looked glum.

"I tell you, we didn't waste any time," the inspector protested. "Two hours after the body was found Groaty and McCarthy were out looking for him."

"And they let him slip through their fingers."

"Slip nothing. The time he slipped was when he left the Thane house night before last. You didn't expect him to stick around and sit on the front doorstep until the police came, did you? Oh, he's slipped all right. He's probably slipped right out of the city."

"You know what puzzles me," Tracy admitted, "is this—if he was going to escape, why didn't he do it immediately instead of delaying a day. Would you mind going over once more the findings of Groaty and McCarthy?"

Herschman suppressed a harassed sigh and patiently repeated his story. "They went around to West Hundred and Fourth Street, the place Thane told us about. The superintendent there said that Spencer had skipped out about three months ago without leaving any address, owing three months' rent and God knows how many bills around the neighborhood. He said they were just as anxious as we were to find out where he is.

"So then Groaty goes down to some of the night clubs where guys like that hang out and finally finds some one that knows him. He's living in an apartment at 15 West Ninety-third Street, just off Central Park West. A big swell place and he's got a butler, or valet, or whatever you want to call him.

"The butler says Spencer came in about four o'clock Tuesday morning and went to bed. Got up at about eleven and went out and he hasn't been back since."

"You may get a line on him when he tries to dispose of the jewels," Tracy suggested hopefully, but Herschman laughed.

"That's likely. People don't steal $200,000 worth of jewelry until they have a reliable fence."

"But you've broadcast the description?"

Herschman nodded "Good one, too. Thane gave it to me yesterday morning just before we left the house. Being a jeweler himself, he knew how to give just the information we wanted. There's one diamond and emerald necklace he says is worth about $50,000, and a string of pearls about $10,000 and a lot of smaller pieces."

They relapsed into gloom and silence again. Presently the district attorney spoke in a voice that was half a groan. "Have you seen the newspapers this morning?"

"Yeah. They're playing it hard. We're in a hole if we don't get our hands on Spencer. I told the reporters that an arrest was expected any moment."

"I suppose you've got men watching Spencer's apartment now?"

"Of course." Herschman could not keep the disgust from his voice.

"What sort of a fellow is the servant?"

"English. Very ruffined and tight-mouthed. We had to pry every word out of him."

"Found Griffis yet?"

"No. He hasn't been at his office since Monday afternoon. He lives at 70 Pierrepont Street on Brooklyn Heights, but be hasn't been there either; I've got men watching both places."

"Another one slipped through your fingers."

"Listen here, Mr. Tracy," said the inspector, now thoroughly aroused, "if you would let me handle this investigation, instead of turning it over to that half-wit—to your brother, there might not be so many slips. Never in all the time I've been a detective have I been up against the situation I'm in now."

The district attorney bridled. He might have his own opinion about his brother, but he allowed no one else the same freedom.

"I think you'll have to admit, Inspector," he said heatedly, "that my brother has proved most valuable. He has certainly opened up a great many more avenues of investigation than were apparent, at first glance. I hardly think you are justified in—"

"Now, now, children, no quarreling, no quarreling. Kiss and make up, and Richard, tell the inspector you're sorry for having such a half-witted brother."

Into the heated, gloomy atmosphere of the room, Spike breezed like a breath of the spring sunshine outside. A gay flower blossomed in his buttonhole, and he swung his walking stick with jaunty abandon. It was evident that he was on his usual good terms with the world. If anything, he seemed more exuberant than ever. With a deft toss he landed his hat on the rack on the opposite side of the room, hooked his stick beneath it, and sprawled into a chair.

"Well," he said looking brightly from one disgruntled face to the other, "what is it that has taken all the sunshine out of your lives today? A new murder?"

"No," the district attorney said shortly, "the old one is quite depressing enough."

"Depressing? To the contrary, I find it frightfully exhilarating. What's new?"

"Nothing. Herschman located Spencer's apartment, but he hasn't been there since yesterday morning, and Griffis hasn't been at his office nor his house since yesterday."

"And so you two are just sitting around being mean to each other."

"Have you anything better to suggest?" said Herschman sarcastically.

"Well," Spike replied with mock apology, "not that I think I'm any great shakes as a raconteur, but possibly since you haven't anything else on your mind, you might like to hear what I've been doing since last I saw your two dear faces."

Herschman merely grunted and Tracy emitted an ill-tempered "Well?"

"Well, first of all," said Spike settling himself more comfortably. "First of all, I lied to you, Richard. I lied. I admit it right out. When I left you yesterday afternoon,, I had no intention whatever of taking a walk. As a matter of fact walking was the furthest from my mind. I had something much more sinister in view.

"I have bad a feeling all along that this case wasn't being conducted properly!" He paused to grin out of the corner of his eyes at Herschman, but the inspector did not even take the trouble to protest the reflection.

"In the first place I may as well confess that I've been disappointed at the way you've gone about things. Not angry, you understand, just terribly, terribly disappointed. You two simply haven't lived up to my idea of what a couple of sleuths ought to be. Not once have either of you examined a footprint through a magnifying glass. You've made no attempt whatever to delve back into the history of the Thanes to discover the family curse which in turn has taken one of each generation ever since the day old Whoosis Thane vowed never—"

"Say lissen, lissen," the inspector interrupted. "What's the idea?"

"I'm coming to that, Inspector, presently. Just give me time. What I'm trying to say is that feeling that the case lacked color I thought I would inject a little into it. Unfortunately I did not have my false whiskers with me but I did the best I could without them. I'm under the impression that false whiskers are what the well-dressed detective wears when he is in the act of—"

"Philip," the district attorney broke in peremptorily, "neither Inspector Herschman nor I have the time or the inclination to listen to your attempts at alleged humor." Spike sighed. "So I see. Ah, well—to put the matter briefly, I went back up to the Fennel apartment house after you left and chatted with the elevator man. Most interesting. He says that Mortimer Fennel and Miss Nina went out together Monday at about eight-thirty and they didn't come back until after one."

He paused. The district attorney who had been drumming impatiently on his desk looked up with a sudden flash of interest.

"But Fennel told us he left the Thane house about nine-thirty and came directly home."

"Exactly," said Spike. "It took him over three and a half hours to cover a distance of perhaps a half a mile. Maybe it took him longer than that. The elevator man goes off duty at one o'clock and he swears that neither Fennel nor Miss Nina came in before then. After one the elevator stops and there is no one in the lobby, you have to walk up."

"Rather—ah—interesting," the district attorney admitted in a guarded manner.

"Rather? You're damn well right it's 'rather' interesting. And it's also 'rather' interesting to realize that Mortimer Fennel could leave his sick wife's bedside more than four hours Monday night for, according to his own testimony, 'just a friendly visit,' and he damn well didn't want to leave her for so much as two minutes when we called on him the following morning."

Herschman said nothing but his manner slowly altered. He was listening now with an ill-concealed eagerness.

"All right. Go on. Then what?" he said impatiently as Spike paused to light a cigarette.

"And now," Spike continued, "I come to the real dirt. After my little chat with the doorman, I went back down to the corner of Eighty-sixth Street and the Drive. You may remember that at that point there is a little park with a lot of trees and shrubbery, just west of the Drive. It slopes down to an iron picket fence, and the New York Central Railroad tracks along the Hudson rim directly beneath.

"Well, I crossed over to the little park and waited, trying my best to look like an idle pedestrian. It got rather boring, especially after three hours' and three very suspicious-looking policemen had passed.

"But presently came four o'clock and I was rewarded. The girl I left behind me, came out of 204 and started down toward the Drive."

The district attorney heaved a sigh of exasperation and disgust, but Spike forestalled whatever words were on his lips.

"No, Richard, you misjudge me absolutely. My intentions were entirely dishonorable. I felt like a beast, backing into the shrubbery and spying on the poor girl as she came across the Drive instead of following my natural and gallant pulse and stepping forth boldly and trying to date her up for the evening."

He paused and blew a contemplative cloud smoke. "As a matter of fact, I wish you'd get this beastly murder business cleared up, so I could do just that thing . . . A blue-eyed brunette. . . ."

"Suppose you go on with your story instead indulging in ridiculous day-dreaming," the district attorney said irritably.

"Let me see, where did I leave myself. Oh, yes, backing into the shrubbery, like the low cad I am. Miss Fennel crossed the Drive and entered the little park. Her manner was designed doubtless to give the impression that she was in the contemplation of Nature and the Palisades but I thought I detected a certain strain about her, as if she were hoping there was no one around to witness what she was about to do.

"She crossed the park and walked down the slope to the iron pickets along the railroad track and waited.

Presently a freight train of open cars filled with sand came along. She waited for a few cars to pass her while she looked around somewhat in the manner of a frightened rabbit.

"I had slunk across the park in her wake and stepped out of sight in another clump of bushes, quite near to her, so I could see plainly what she was doing."

He paused and smiled benignly on his two listeners.

"And would you believe it, that beautiful girl pulled out of her handbag one of the most murderous-looking revolvers I ever saw in my life."

Both the inspector and the district attorney were sitting forward in their chairs now.

"And what did she do with it?" Herschman snapped.

"Why," said Spike calmly, "she threw it into one of the cars passing below and it was buried in the nice clean sand and carted off to God knows wherever the train was going."

Herschman sprang from his chair and glared at him.

"Young fellow, are you telling the truth or is this your idea of a joke?"

"Really, Inspector, you misjudge my sense of humor."

"Would you get up and swear to that in court?"

"Well, being, as I have already pointed out, a low cad, I would if I were forced to, but if you don't mind, I'd really rather not. Miss Fennel, you know, is an extraordinarily charming girl and I wouldn't like—"

"Shut up!" Herschman barked and reached for the telephone with an excited gesture.

"Now don't," Spike cautioned, "be impolite to me, Inspector, because I might get mad and not tell you the rest of my story and it's really rather intriguing."

But Herschman had his own office on the wire and he paid no heed to the warning "Mallory?"

"Yes."

"Get in touch with the New York Center freight yards along Riverside Drive immediately and check up on all shipments of sand that went north yesterday afternoon.

Find out the destination of every car and tell them no matter where the sand is, it's to be held for inspection before unloading. Then get men out after it. Search every car for a gun. Now have you got it straight?"

"Yes, sir."

"Well, then, hurry. Don't lose a minute." He jammed the receiver down on the hook and started out the door. "I'm going up to question this Fennel woman, and I'd rather do it alone," he said curtly.

"But, Inspector—" Spike too had risen from his chair and laid a detaining hand on Herman's arm. "I really think it would be to your advantage to hear my babblings to the end."

"I'm going to see Nina Fennel and I'm going now."

"Oh, really?" Spike's hand tightened about the inspector's arm in a firm grip, and he slowly pulled him back into the room. "If you go now, you won't hear the end of my story. And anyway, Miss Fennel had a very fatiguing day yesterday and I have no doubt she is still asleep."

"Lissen here, young fellow," Herschman turned on Spike with an ominous look in his eyes. "Are you trying to keep anything from my—"

"To the contrary, I'm doing my best to tell all, to bare my soul, and you won't listen."

Herschman shook off the restraining hand, hesitated a moment and then seated himself once more.

"Well?" he snapped.

"Well," Spike continued, "after Miss Fennel parked her gun, she retraced her steps across the little park and hailed a taxi and drove downtown, with me in hot pursuit in another cab. She stopped at an obscure little restaurant over on Second Avenue, near Fourteenth Street, and went inside and took a table and began crumbling bread, and drawing figures on the tablecloth with her fork and looking at her watch and all in all acting like a very nervous woman.

"Apparently it was a prearranged rendezvous of some sort because presently a young fellow came in and sat down at her table, and they went into a huddle with their foreheads together looking mutually distressed. Unfortunately I am not a lip reader, but I fancy that she told him something that surprised him greatly and then he told her something that made her start and grip the edges of the table, and by-and-by after they had ordered about three dollars worth of food and hadn't eaten three cents worth, she got up and left."

Spike paused again, apparently for breath.

"And you followed her?" the inspector asked.

"No, I didn't."

"You didn't?"

"No. As a matter of fact, I was beginning to be a little tired of my false whisker role, and quite a bit ashamed of myself, spying on the poor girl, so I remained in the restaurant and kept my eye on the boy friend.

Herschman threw up his hands in outraged disgust.

"Oh, my God!"

"Really, Inspector, you shouldn't take things so hard. Bad for the blood pressure. And anyway the boy friend was fully as interesting a Miss Fennel.

"While he was waiting for the waiter to bring his check, I sauntered over to his table and just casually dropped into conversation with him. Very delightful fellow. We got on famously together. As a matter of fact we got on so well that I invited him up to my apartment for the night."

He paused and selected another cigarette from his case and lit it leisurely.

"Well," said Herschman impatiently, "who was this Fennel woman's boy friend, and what's his name."

"His name," said Spike, "is Tommy Spencer."

VII. "Night Club Sheik Held"

FOR a moment neither the district attorney nor the inspector said a word. Then they spoke simultaneously.

"Tommy Spencer?"

Spike nodded. "Tommy Spencer. Cecily Thane's boy friend of the night before last. We had quite a long talk together. Very interesting."

"Where's he now?" The words fairly shot from Herschman.

Spike nodded toward the anteroom. "Out there. No—" he protested as Herschman started toward the door. "He's quite safe. I tipped off two of your officers to watch him. As a matter of fact I think Tommy's keeping something from me, and it irks me. I wouldn't like him to get away before we found out what it is."

Suddenly Herschman came over and stood squarely in front of Spike and glowered down at him. "Look here, young fellow," he said, "you think you're pretty bright, don't you."

"Well," Spike grinned disarmingly, "don't you?"

"No. You've just got plain damn fools' luck."

"Suppose," said the district attorney in a placating voice from which the surprise had not entirely disappeared. "Suppose, Philip, you tell us a little bit more about your evening with Spencer."

"I'm afraid there's not much more to tell. I was perfectly frank with him after I scraped up the acquaintance. I told him I was the district attorney's brother and that I was—ah—interested in the Thane case and would he be so kind as to tell me all he knew about it."

"And he did?"

"Well, I have a feeling that up to a certain point he repaid my frankness with frankness."

"Just had him eating out of your hand, didn't you?" Herschman's voice was heavy with sarcasm.

"No," Spike admitted, "I would hardly go far as to say that. There were moments in our conversation when sheer physical force was all that kept Tommy by my side. Fortunately I'm about fifty pounds heavier than he."

"Well, go on with your story."

"One rather interesting point, he did clear up. He was not involved in the Schlockenhass case."

"Oh, he wasn't, wasn't he? And how do you know that?"

"Because he told me so."

"And you believe him?"

"His explanation was most logical. He said that his unfortunate arrest was due to a misapprehension on your part as to his true character."

"He told you that?"

"Not in precisely that way," Spike temporized. "His exact words were, if I remember correctly —'That goddam, lousy Herschman couldn't get it through his wooden head that just because the old girl paid me to let her step on my feet, I wasn't the one that bumped her off.'"

"What else did he have to say for himself?"

"He said that you had almost ruined his career. That's why he had to change his name. And he told me what he'd been doing since he left the Thane house Monday night. Quite open and frank about it. At least up to a certain point. From then on—Well, I don't know. Really I would like to get an expert opinion of the lad's story from the combined legal and police minds of New York County."

"What's the story he told you?"

"Let's have him in and let him tell it himself."

Herschman nodded in agreement and the district attorney called the outside office on the telephone. Almost immediately the door opened.

The cold details of the police record card were hardly an adequate description of William Preston alias Tommy Spencer. As the slight, dark young man stood in the doorway there was an air about him that was undeniably attractive—an attraction made up of good looks and an almost pathetic helplessness—a type that is extremely intriguing to women. But it was plain that he was striving now to put up a bold front. His eyes as he met those of the district attorney and the inspector were apprehensive but defiant; his movements were of the nervous, jerky type peculiar to young men who sleep in the daytime and spend their nights drinking and dancing.

"Well," he said with exaggerated coolness, "here I am"

"Back again," said Herschman The inspector motioned him to a chair and looked at him with narrowed eyes in the manner of a sidewalk cop eyeing a crook from the morning line-up. Then his jaw set and he jammed his hands into his pockets. "You know what you're here for," he snapped.

"Yes, I know." He answered with a surly bravado that was obviously assumed. "You think I bumped off Mrs. Thane just like you thought I bumped off Mrs. Schlockenhass."

"Suppose you cut out the fresh talk and tell me what you know. Where did you and the Thane woman go Monday night?"

"We went down to the Club Paradis and had dinner and danced and we came home about eleven-thirty and went up to her sitting room on the second floor."

"It isn't usual, is it, in your line of business to get in at such respectable hours. I thought women paid you to keep 'em out late."

"Yes, but Monday night some special friends of mine were giving a party, and I told her I could only give her half the evening. It had been a party that was arranged for another night and then they suddenly changed the date. And she was a good egg, so she said it was O.K."

"Well, then, what did you do when you brought her home and got her up in the sitting room?"

"We had a couple of cocktails and then I left."

"What time?"

But before Spencer could answer, the inspector's question Spike broke in with one of his own. "Mind telling again, Tommy, in just what position Mrs. Thane was the last time you saw her."

"She was on the chaise longue."

"And she was, I take it, still alive and well?"

"Say, how many times do I have to tell you that I'm not the one that did the shooting?"

"It's distressingly evident, Tommy, that you're not familiar with that famous line of Shakespeare's, 'Methinks he doth protest too much.' You really should read—"

But he was cut short by a glowering glance from Herschman.

"What time did you leave the Thane house Monday night?" the inspector put in.

"Oh, I don't know. About half an hour later, I guess."

"And then what did you do?"

"I went back down to the Paradis and stayed there till four o'clock; and then I went home and went to bed and slept till eleven—and if you don't believe it you can ask the man I've got work—" He broke off suddenly in confusion.

"We have already."

"Wha—what did he tell you?" There was a sudden tenseness in his voice

"Never mind what he told us. I'm asking the questions, not you. Then what did you do?"

Spencer hesitated. "I went for a walk."

"You went for a walk?" Herschman's voice was sarcastic. "Your morning constitutional, I suppose."

"No, just a walk. Can't a fellow take a walk?"

"That depends on where he walks. Where'd you go?"

"Oh, just around—just along the Drive."

"You didn't just happen to walk down to Eighty-sixth Street and see Miss Fennel?"

At the mention of Nina Fennel's name there was just the flash of an eyelid, an almost imperceptible tightening of the jaw, and when he spoke his voice was just a shade more defiant and surly.

"No I didn't see Miss Fennel until four o'clock yesterday afternoon."

"And what were you seeing her for?"

"I had a date with her?"

"What for?"

"What do you mean, 'what for?'"

"Under the circumstances, Mr. Spencer," the district attorney's voice broke smoothly into the swift staccato of questions and answers, "it would be best if you were to state frankly just what your business with Miss Fennel was."

"I didn't have any 'business' with her. It was just a date. My God, haven't you ever had a date?"

"Don't attempt to delve so far back into ancient history, old thing," Spike put in. Then turning to Herschman and the district attorney. "I think what he means to say is that his engagement was purely a social one for the purpose of tea and conversation."

"Yes, that's it."

"What did you talk about" Herschman went on.

"Oh, different things?"

"What, for instance?"

"Oh—I dunno—people we know—things like that?"

"You didn't happen to be talking about Mrs. Thane?"

"Yes, we did talk about her. We spent most of the time talking about her. Why shouldn't we? After all if it hadn't been for Mrs. Thane, I'd never met Ni—Miss Fennel."

"Oh, so Mrs. Thane introduced you to Miss Fennel. When?"

"One night about three months ago at a night club. Miss Fennel was with a party at another table and she came over and spoke to Mrs. Thane and we were introduced."

"Tommy," Spike broke in, "let me get this just straight. Miss Fennel came over and spoke to Mrs. Thane first and Mrs. Thane introduced you."

"Yes."

"And since then you've known her quite well?"

"Well, sort of."

"Would it be impertinent of me to inquire whether she is one of your—ah—customers?"

"No. Nina Fennel doesn't have to pay men to take her around." It was evident from Spencer's voice that he was slightly contemptuous of his clientele.

"How did she seem the first time she met you? What did her feelings seem to be toward you?"

Spencer lowered his eyes and fumbled with one of the buttons on his coat. "Why she seemed to—well, sort of like me right off. I got a man I know to take care of Mrs. Thane and I went over and danced with Ni—Miss Fennel and she—well—uh—"

"She made it plain that your attentions were acceptable?"

"Yes, that's it."

"I don't see what this has got to do with the case," Herschman broke in irritably.

"Probably hasn't, Inspector," Spike admitted. "Just a quaint idea of mine. I'm so interested in people, you know."

"How often have you been seeing Miss Fennel since then?" the inspector went on.

"Oh, about once or twice a week."

"Just 'dates'?"

"Just dates."

"And after she left you in the restaurant yesterday afternoon, you went with Mr. Tracy here to his apartment for the night?"

Spencer nodded.

"And you're sure you didn't do anything but just walk yesterday afternoon?"

"Yes."

"Up and down the Drive?"

"Yes, up and down the Drive."

"Are you in the habit of walking from eleven-thirty in the morning until four in the afternoon?"

"No, but I had a bad head on me from the party the night before and I wanted to walk it off."

"You didn't have lunch any place?"

"Guys in my business don't eat lunch."

"And when had you made this 'date' with Miss Fennel?"

"I stopped in at a drug store and called her up and told her to meet me?"

"About what time did you telephone Miss Fennel," Spike broke in.

"Oh, I don't know."

"Rack the old brains and let me have the exact hour."

"Oh, maybe—two—three o'clock."

"And from where?"

"United Cigar Store on Seventy-second Street and Broadway."

"And you told her to meet you down on Second Avenue at four o'clock."

"Yes."

"Your witness, Inspector."

"You bet he's my witness," said Herschman, "and I'm so fond of him that I'm going to hold him as a material witness—without bail."

He turned a triumphant smile on the district attorney.

"Didn't I tell you I'd make an arrest any moment?"

Spike grinned and said nothing.

VIII. BRIBERY AND CORRUPTION!

AS Spike rode uptown in a taxi he scanned the fresh ink of the latest afternoon tab which heralded the arrest of Tommy Spencer.

"Night Club Sheik Held"

And underneath the inevitable picture—"Tommy Spencer, boy-friend of Cecily Thane and the last person known to have seen her alive, being taken to the Tombs by Inspector Herschman. Story on page 2."

There followed a carefully abridged account of the morning's events at Police Headquarters. Just how and where the elusive Spencer had been apprehended was not quite plain, but the obvious inference was that Inspector Herschman, like the true servant of the people that he was, had not been idle.

"I see," Spike mused as his eye came to the bottom of the column, "that in his elation at making an arrest the inspector has forgotten about Nina. I'm afraid he doesn't realize that for publicity purposes the female of the species is more effective than the male. However, far be it from me to bandy a lady's name about with tabloid reporters—God bless their bloody hearts."

The taxi stopped at 15 West Ninety-third Street and he got out. The apartment house which he entered was one of the newer buildings that had recently sprung up near Central Park West—a rather gaudy edifice with a lobby inhabited by a mixture of modernistic divans, Renaissance refectory tables and an imposing looking door man.

The apartment of Tommy Spencer was on the fifteenth floor, a rather luxurious suite of four rooms with a magnificent view overlooking the Park. The door was opened by a servant.

"You, I take it," said Spike as he stood on the threshold, "are Murray."

"Yes, sir."

Nothing more correct in appearance or demeanor had ever come out of an English servants' hall than Murray. It was rather a shock to find one of his patent aristocracy serving a professional dancing man. Anything less than a duke seemed beneath him.

"I have an unfortunate message from your master," Spike explained. "Here," and he thrust the newspaper into the servant's hand as he brushed passed him through the small reception hall into the living room.

It was a disorderly place, and it was apparent that it had not been cleaned recently. Murray's impeccability did not, it was plain, extend to the actual performance of his duties. Spike surveyed it carefully as he waited for the man to finish his glance at the headlines.

"Mr. Spencer is in prison?"

"Unfortunate, isn't it?"

"Most unfortunate, sir, but I was expecting it. The gentlemen from the police department were here yesterday and were most curious."

Spike slumped into a chair and took out his cigarette case.

"By the way, what was the story you told them? You see, I'm one of the gentlemen from the police department myself. I am the brother of the district attorney and I am assisting in the investigation."

"I only answered their questions, sir."

"Well," said Spike as he flicked the ash from his cigarette into a near-by ash tray, "suppose you answer a few of mine."

"I am sorry, sir, but I fear there is nothing more that I can add. We went quite thoroughly into the matter."

"Yes?" Spike's voice rose in that curious inflection which turns an affirmative into a negative.

"Yes. sir."

"As I understand it, Mr. Spencer came home at about four o'clock Monday morning and went to bed and got up at eleven."

"Yes, sir."

"Do you know by any chance whether he possessed a gun?"

"I couldn't say as to that, sir."

"You are his valet, aren't you, and you look after his clothes and go through his dresser drawers, don't you?"

"Yes, sir."

"And have you ever seen a gun anywhere in the apartment?"

"I couldn't say as to that, sir."

"But you remember what you've seen and what you haven't."

"I don't recall, sir."

The good-humored air which was part of Spike's habitual expression slowly faded, and a calculating look came into his eyes, carefully veiled by a disarming casualness.

"Working long for Mr. Spencer?"

"Four months, sir."

"You're not by any chance the John Murray that used to valet the Duke of Westbury."

"No, sir. My name is Angus Isaac Murray, and in London I was with Sir Jordan Henley."

"Quite a bit of mixed ancestry?"

"Yes, sir. My mother was Scotch and, my father was English and one of my grandfathers was Hebrew."

Spike smiled. "Well, that makes things easier."

"Beg pardon, sir?"

"I mean I find your family history highly diverting. Tell me more. How come you're now in a position which is so obviously below your talents."

"Misfortunes overtake us all, sir. I was so foolish as to be lured to New York by an American gentleman who wished a valet. We disagreed at a most unfortunate time—soon after I had dropped a bit too much at the Pimlico races. In my extremity, I was forced to take the first thing that was offered until I could get back to England."

"But surely in four months you could save enough to pay your passage home."

"No, sir."

"Pardon me, Murray, if I seem to intrude upon a rather delicate matter—but are your wages paid up to date."

"No, sir."

"Mr. Spencer was not in the habit of paying his bills promptly?"

"No, sir. That has been one of the most distressing features of my work here."

"How much does he owe you?"

"Two hundred dollars, sir."

"Why do you remain?"

"I'm only staying until I can collect what is owed me. Mr. Spencer said last week that he would raise quite a large sum of money soon."

"And the rent on the apartment?"

"It is two months, overdue, sir."

A slow smile twisted up the corner of Spike's mouth. With a leisurely gesture he drew his bill fold from his inside pocket and selected a ten and two yellow-backed twenties. When he had replaced the wallet he tapped the folded bills meditatively on his palm with a significant gesture.

"You know, Murray," he said, "I don't believe that the chaps who were here yesterday were very thorough. I have a feeling that you and I, perhaps, will—ah— understand each other better."

For a moment the valet remained silent, his eyes on the tapping bills. Then he spoke without the shadow of a change in his expression or demeanor.

"Yes, sir. Quite."

Spike's eyes under half-opened lids slowly felt their way about the littered room.

"When did you clean here last?"

"Monday, sir. Monday afternoon."

"Did Mr. Spencer by any chance have any visitors on Monday night."

"Yes, sir."

"And who were they?"

"There was only one, sir—a lady."

"Her name?"

"I don't know it, sir."

"A young lady?"

"Yes, sir."

"Was this her first visit here?"

"No, she had been once before. She was here last Sunday afternoon for tea."

"And at what time did she come Monday night?"

"At about a quarter to one."

"A quarter to one." Spike sat forward in his chair. "Are you sure of that?"

"Yes, sir. I always make it a point to note the time of visitors so that I can make a proper report."

"Suppose you just go ahead and tell me about her without my questions."

"Well, sir, she asked for Mr. Spencer and I told her he would not return until probably early in the morning. She came in and said that she wished to write a note to him. I left her in here alone, and in a few moments she called me and gave me the note and asked me to give it to Mr. Spencer as soon as he got up in the morning. She was most insistent. And then she left."

"What was her manner?"

"She seemed—ah—somewhat upset. I would say very upset."

"And in the morning you delivered the note to Mr. Spencer?"

"Yes, sir."

"You don't by any chance know what was in it? You didn't—ah—just happen to read it?"

Murray hesitated and his glance went to the bills in Spike's hand. "No, sir," he said firmly.

Again there was a pause. And again Spike reached slowly for his wallet and drew out two more yellow twenties and a ten and placed them with the hundred.

"Rack your brains, Murray. Are you quite sure you can't recall?"

"Well," he temporized and went through the facial gestures which usually accompany a racking of the brains. "As a matter of fact, it was, I believe, something like this, although I could not swear to the exact wording, of course: 'Tommy, Something terrible has happened. I must see you right away. Telephone me in the morning.'"

"And the signature?"

"I couldn't make it out. It was just a single letter, quite illegible."

Spike appeared to digest these facts for a few moments in silence. Then again the slow gesture to the inside pocket, and again two more twenties and a ten.

"Concentrate on this gun business, Murray. Are you quite sure that you never saw a gun in Mr. Spencer's possession"

Again a short pause while Murray searched his memory.

"Well—yes, sir, I have"

"He keeps one here in the apartment"

"Yes, sir."

"You don't happen to know what kind of a gun?"

"A .38 caliber Colt, I believe."

"Did you by any chance notice whether he took it with him Monday night before he went to Mrs. Thane's."

"No, sir, I didn't."

"Quite sure?" Spike gave a decisive flick with the bills.

"Quite sure, sir, but—"

"But what?"

"It is not in its usual resting place now."

"And where is it?"

"I don't know, sir. Mr. Spencer took it out with him yesterday morning when he left the apartment."

"How did he act just before he went out? Was he—ah—just what was his manner?"

"Well, sir, at eleven o'clock he summoned me and asked for the afternoon paper and his breakfast."

"The *afternoon* paper?"

"Yes, sir. You see Mr. Spencer says that the morning news is stale by the time he is up—he seldom rises before eleven—so he has the early edition of the afternoon paper delivered here in the morning."

"What paper?"

"This one." With a fastidiously offended gesture, Murray picked up from the reading table the glaring tabloid which Spike had brought with him and held it between his thumb and forefinger.

"You, I take it," said Spike with a slight grin, "read the *Times*."

"Yes, sir."

"And after you had given Mr. Spencer the paper, he ate his breakfast and then went out."

"No, sir. He went out immediately. He didn't touch his breakfast."

"Is he in the habit of going without food in the morning?"

"No, sir. It's the first time I've ever known it to happen."

"You have no—ah—theory, have you, Murray, to account for his sudden distaste for food."

"I think it was something he read in the paper that upset him."

"No doubt. Or perhaps it was the young lady's note. Did he read it before or after he read the paper."

"I couldn't say, sir. I brought them both in at the same time and then left the room."

"Did he telephone before he went out?"

"No, sir."

"Or say where he was going?"

"No, sir. He appeared in a great hurry."

"Well, Murray, you've been most helpful."

Spike rose from his chair and laid the $150 in bills on the reading table and picked up his stick.

"And Mr. Spencer's message?" Murray reminded him.

"Well, as a matter of fact, he's in need of clean socks, shuts and B.V.D's I suggested that I drop by and get them for him, but he seemed positively appalled at the prospect of having me get chummy with you. He told me to get them at a haberdashery, so just to keep his mind at peace on that score at least, I'll do as he asked."

"Yes, sir." For a moment the shadow of a comprehending smile lighted up Murray's correct countenance.

At the door Spike paused suddenly as if he had just remembered something.

"By the way, did you happen to notice whether the young lady was a blue-eyed brunette?"

"No, sir. Her hair was tucked up under her hat, and I am not in the habit of noticing lady's eyes."

"You should make it a point to do so, Murray. You miss a lot."

"Yes, sir."

"Perhaps you remember some of her conversation, though—the Sunday afternoon she had tea here."

Murray hesitated. Slowly he reached for the pile of bills on the reading table and counted them through, folded them and put them in his pocket.

"I'm afraid not, sir," he replied firmly.

"But surely you can tell me what sort of a person she was. What I mean to say, was she like most of Mr. Spencer's friends?"

"No, sir. If I may say so, she was greatly superior. Most of Mr. Spencer's friends are of a class to which I am not accustomed."

"In other words she was a lady."

"Quite, sir"

"And I suppose you served the tea?"

"Yes, sir."

"And now and again you caught snatches of their, conversation?"

"Well, occasionally."

"Do you recall any of it?"

"Well, sir, I—" He left the sentence trailing in mid-air.

"Strain your brain just this once more, Murray," Spike persisted, and as he spoke he crossed the room and laid a fifty-dollar bill on the reading table. "Surely, you found something diverting in this particular visitor's conversation."

"Well, at the time, sir, I didn't think. so—but—"

"But subsequent events, have added interest to her remarks?"

"Yes, sir."

"Suppose you tell me about it."

"Well, Mr. Spencer summoned me to bring in the tea and I caught the name of Mrs. Thane. I got the impression that the young lady was somewhat bitter. If I remember exactly she said, 'I've known her for fifteen years and hated her for seven of them. Ever since—' At that point unfortunately I left the room." He paused.

"But you returned?" Spike prodded him gently on.

"Yes, sir. About a half hour later to take away the tea things. I would not swear, you understand, that they were still talking about Mrs. Thane. At least I didn't hear her name actually mentioned. But the young lady had hardly touched her tea and she was still saying something about hating. She said—" He hesitated, earnest in his efforts to be accurate.

"She said, 'I hate her so much, I'll kill her some day.'"

IX. NINA FENNEL IS "PERFECTLY FRANK"

AN hour later at Police Headquarters Spike faced an irate district attorney and a highly incensed inspector.

"But why should this Murray withhold information from the legally authorized authorities and give it to you?" Tracy sputtered. "Groaty and McCarthy questioned him for an hour. I've a mind to have him arrested for obstructing justice."

"I think you're a bit hard on him," Spike defended. "And probably he answered all their questions right enough. They evidently didn't ask the right ones—in the right way. He has the correct English servant's dislike of the police and sensational publicity. But fortunately for us, his Scotch mother and his Jewish grandfather made it difficult for him to resist the lure of a good bargain. Your men appealed to the Murray of him and I to the Angus Isaac."

"Why it's bribery," Tracy persisted. "Pure bribery."

"Not at all, I was simply paying him his back wages. Two hundred dollars was the exact amount. As a matter of fact, just before I left I gave him another fifty and intimated that God had still more good things in store for him if he stuck around and didn't beat it off to dear old London on the next boat. I thought perhaps you'd like to confirm what I've just been telling you, Inspector."

"Say lissen, young fellow, what right have you got going up there and questioning state's witnesses without authority from me?"

"Surely, Inspector, it isn't within your power to prevent two private citizens from having a clubby little chat with each other."

"Well, I'm telling you this right now, you—"

"Don't! It's just possible that I might get temperamental and refuse to finish my story. And really, you know, I picked up two little souvenirs which I think you might be interested in."

"Get this straight. I'm not interested—". With difficulty Herschman stemmed the flow of his wrath as he realized that he was most decidedly interested. When he spoke again it was with sullen capitulation. "Well, go ahead, what have you got?"

"But first of all, Inspector, let me register my hearty agreement with you on one point. I think you were quite right in being skeptical of Tommy's devotion to Nature and the joys of walking in the open air. I have a feeling that somewhere in the course of that walk he disposed of the gun which Murray assured me he took with him when he left his apartment yesterday morning, because he didn't have it last night when I took him home with me."

Herschman grew slightly mollified and Spike went on.

"Number one of my little souvenirs is this." He took from his pocket a tabloid newspaper and unfolded its gaudy face. "The good old *Evening Graphic*, the only paper which carried the news of Cecily Thane's murder in the first edition, the paper which Tommy Spencer has brought to his apartment every morning at eleven o'clock."

"Well, what of it?"

"Frankly it may be just a coincidence, just another proof of the world-beating qualities of my favorite sheet. And then again— Well, I'll confess, I don't know.

"Here's something more definite, though." From his cigarette case, he drew forth a half smoked cigarette, one end ringed with heavy carmine rouge. "As soon as I palmed this souvenir from the ash tray beside the most comfortable chair in Tommy's apartment, I had a feeling that Murray had not opened his heart and told all to my predecessors. Hence my rather generous expense account."

Herschman bent forward and examined the butt. "The Fennel girl!" He gasped in spite of himself.

"Miss Fennel, Inspector," Spike reproved him. "Would you mind, Richard, handing over the other six in this set?"

From a drawer in his desk Tracy brought forth a small pasteboard box and opened it and Spike put the cigarette which he had just brought beside the others.

"A perfect match."

"Well," said Herschman, "where does that get us?"

"Let me remind you that a young lady visited Spencer's apartment at one o'clock Tuesday morning and that Murray assured me that he had not cleaned the room or emptied the ash trays since. I think therefore that we may assume that she smoked this cigarette. The rouge on it corresponds exactly with that on the three that were found in the Thane sitting room and with the one which I myself saw Nina Fennel light.

"The conclusion is fairly obvious. Nina Fennel was in Cecily Thane's sitting room Monday night and she was at Tommy Spencer's apartment early Tuesday morning— writing a rather desperate-sounding note.

"Less than forty-eight hours before Cecily Thane was killed Nina Fennel threatened to kill some one and I have a strong suspicion that she referred to Cecily Thane. And less than twenty-four hours after Cecily Thane is killed Nina Fennel is seen throwing a gun into a passing freight car of sand.

"I think it's all frightfully intriguing and I rather imagine that Miss Fennel is our next move."

"*Our* next move?" Herschman rose with a determined glint in his eye and started for the door. But once again Spike forestalled him and laid a firm grip on his arm.

"Inspector, I don't like your ironic emphasis on the 'our.' Surely you won't deny me the pleasure of an interview with the only blue-eyed brunette I've ever known who wasn't married to a man heavier than I?"

As the district attorney, the inspector and Spike stood in the dark hall outside the Fennel apartment, Spike cast a beseeching glance at Herschman.

"Remember, Inspector," he threatened, even as he implored, "even on such slight acquaintance, I have grown tremendously fond of Miss Fennel, and it would upset me no end if you handled her roughly."

"I know my business," the inspector grumbled and pressed the buzzer.

This time it was a maid who answered the ring, a slatternly young person dragging a dirty dust mop in her wake. She ushered them into the front room in silence and not until they were seated did she speak.

"Miss Fennel and Mr. Fennel's both with Mrs. Fennel. She's awful sick and they said I wasn't to disturb them unless it was important."

"It is important—very important," and the inspector fixed such a stern eye on the girl that she turned and hurried down the hall making a loud slip-slopping with her loose bedroom slippers.

In a few moments, Nina Fennel came into the room. She was wearing the same dress that she had worn the previous day. It was crumpled and her hair was mussed as if, perhaps, she had not had her clothes off all night. There were deep circles under her eyes and her face seemed to droop with fatigue and anxiety. Yet strangely enough she seemed even more striking looking than she had the day before. It was as if impending tragedy had lent her a passionate sort of strength and beauty.

As she stood in the doorway and looked at the three men she seemed to stiffen in every muscle. Her expression was suddenly just a shade too determinedly matter-of-fact.

"My mother—" she began but the district attorney broke in.

"Yes, I know, Miss Fennel. I am most sorry, but it is absolutely essential that I talk to you—you and your father. This is Inspector Herschman of the police department and there are certain matters he would like to go over with you."

"Very well." She came and sat down and seemed to surrender herself to the three men.

"I would like to talk to your father too, Miss Fennel," Herschman reminded her.

"I'm sorry but that is quite impossible. My mother is very, very low and one of us must be at her bedside constantly. Won't I do just as well?"

'I'm afraid not. I want to see your father too."

Nina Fennel did not move an inch, or lift so much as an eyebrow, but somehow she seemed slowly to become as steel, unbending, inflexible.

"I'm sorry," she said in the same level voice, "but it is quite impossible."

"But if I insist?"

"But you—you can't." She seemed beset by a sudden panic and her voice grew pleading, imploring. "Please— don't you understand? It may be my mother's last minute on earth—even now. She asks for him constantly. You mustn't drag him away. You can't."

Herschman opened his mouth to speak but before the words could come out, Spike cut in in a quiet tone.

"May I suggest, Inspector, that we accede to Miss Fennel's suggestion and use her as a proxy for her father?"

Herschman glared in Spike's direction, but the young man went on, unperturbed. "There are a number of things about which I am sure she will be even more helpful than her father."

The inspector grunted and chewed the edge of his lip. It was plain that he was wishing that Spike were taking a walk in Central Park or perhaps even better, in Hyde Park. That would mean the whole Atlantic Ocean between them. But finally he conquered his feelings and with no particular good grace turned once more toward Nina Fennel.

"Suppose, Miss Fennel," he said, "you tell me just what you were doing last Monday night."

For a moment there was a dead silence in the room. Nina Fennel sat staring straight before her with her lips in a tense line. Then she turned suddenly and faced the inspector.

"I was at Mrs. Thane's." Herschman started slightly at the suddenness of her capitulation. The straightforward answer where he had expected evasion had the effect of a slap in the face on him. He blinked and Nina Fennel smiled slightly. "That is what you wanted to know wasn't it?"

"Yes—but—"

"Won't you please go ahead with your questions. I want to get back to my mother as quickly as possible."

"What were you doing there?"

Again she paused, considering her answer carefully. "Inspector," she said finally, "I am going to be perfectly frank with you. Yesterday when the district attorney and this gentleman were here," and she indicated Spike, "they talked to my father, but they did not take the trouble to question me. They questioned only my father and he answered them truthfully."

"But that's not answering my question What were you doing at Mrs. Thane's and what time were you there and how did you get in?"

"I went with my father—"

"You went into the house with your father?"

"No, I went to the house with my father. He went in and a little later he let me in."

"About what time was that?"

"Eight-thirty, perhaps nine."

"And what did you and your father do while you were at Mrs. Thane's?"

"We sat there for a while—perhaps fifteen or twenty minutes. And then he went home."

"And you?"

"I remained."

"For how long?"

"An hour—perhaps longer. I'm not just sure."

"And what were you doing while you were there?"

"Just sitting. Sitting and smoking."

Spike looked triumphantly in the direction of Herschman, but the inspector went on doggedly. "And after you left?"

"I took a walk. Quite a long walk."

"You just walked. Where did you walk to? Did you go to any one's house or apartment?"

"No, I just walked. It—it was a nice night and I felt the need of air, so I just took a walk."

"And what time did you get home?"

"I'm not sure, but it was sometime after one. The elevator in the hall stops at one, and I had to walk upstairs, so it must have been after one."

"What, Miss Fennel, was the—uh—purpose of your visit to the Thane house?"

"As my father told the district attorney, yesterday, just a social call. Mrs. Thane had been kind enough to write to my mother and inquire about her, so we just dropped in for a moment."

"But why was it that you did not enter the house at the same time as your father?"

"I had an errand to do at the drug store on the corner and I told him to go on. I was a little longer than I had expected to be."

"And who let you in?"

"My father. He didn't want to bring the maid up from downstairs again to answer the door, so when he saw me coming, he opened it before I had even a chance to ring."

"I see. And then you and your father went upstairs and sat there fifteen or twenty minutes and he left."

"Yes."

"But why didn't you leave with him?"

"He got tired of waiting. The maid told me that she wasn't sure just where Mr. Thane was, and that he might be in any minute, so I thought I'd wait a little while longer."

"Miss Fennel, how long have you and your father and your mother been friends with the Thanes?"

"Ever since I can remember. Ever since I was quite a little girl."

"Did Mrs. Thane come here often to see your mother, now that she is so ill?"

"No. She was a very busy woman and then sickness depresses her so. She often wrote notes and sent flowers."

"Your mother has been ill long?"

"My mother has been confined to a wheel chair for the last twenty-three years. But it is only recently that she has been so seriously ill. She had a bad spell early Tuesday morning."

Herschman settled himself back in his chair and looked steadily at Nina Fennel for a moment, the corners of his mouth, turned up in just the suggestion of a smile. It was the expression one often remarks on the face of a cat, surveying an unsuspecting mouse, just the moment before it reaches out with its clawed paw.

"Tell me, Miss Fennel," he said at length, "do you happen to know a you—"

"Wait!" It was Spike breaking in. "Listen !" He held up his hand for silence "They're calling you, Miss Fennel, down there," and he pointed in the direction of the hail leading into the sick room.

Nina Fennel sprang from her chair and rushed down the hall, her face suddenly overspread with dread and fright.

Once outside the apartment house, Herschman let go on Spike. "Say, what the hell did you have to go butting in with a phony remark about some one calling, just when I was about to show that dame up."

"Exactly, Inspector, exactly," said Spike smiling blithely. "I knew you were going to do just that little thing and that's why the hell."

Herschman surveyed him with a look that said plainly enough "It's only the fact that you're the district attorney's brother that keeps me from throwing you into the Hudson River with a five hundred-pound boulder tied to your feet."

But Spike went right ahead, disregarding the murder that was in Herschman's heart "You see, old thing," he explained, "when a woman says, 'I'm going to be perfectly frank with you' you can bet your sweet life she's preparing a whole bushel of whoppers. And Miss Nina Fennel, despite her many other superior charms, is all too like her sisters in this respect She lied like hell. She was 'quite frank' about all those things which she knew we could check her up on. Her arrival at the Fennel's—her return home—that sort of thing. But she didn't know that we had already had a little tête-a-tête with Tommy Spencer's butler so she went right ahead with her lies and thought she was putting it over on us."

"Then why not tell her so right to her face"

"And put her on her guard? No, no. She thinks she has fooled us completely. She won't be so careful about watching her step!"

For the second time that day Herschman retreated into the mumbled silence of defeat.

"And it strikes me very forcibly," said Spike, "that she had rehearsed everything she told us. It flowed off too glibly."

"Say, lissen," said Herschman, "I thought you were gone on this dame, and now you seem absolutely pleased that we've got the goods on her."

"Pleased? Inspector! And you think you are an accurate reader of the human countenance. I'm torn— simply torn within. For the second time in my life I am suffering bitter disappointment. The other blue-eyed brunette, as I have already pointed out, had a husband forty pounds heavier than I. And this one—well, it looks very much like she may be a murderer." Spike blew a disconsolate cloud of cigarette smoke into the air. Then he

added with philosophic resignation: "Still, I suppose all
women have their drawbacks. You just have to take them
as they come."

"Yes, and another drawback she's going to have,"
Herschman put the last word to the argument, "is a cop
watching that apartment house from now on, and trailing
her wherever she goes."

X. Mr. Shansky Defends His Reputation

ON Thursday morning, the third day after the murder of Cecily Thane, Herschman entered the office of the district attorney and slammed the door viciously behind him. Tracy at his desk, scanning the morning papers with an harassed air, looked up quickly.

"Well?" he said irritably.

"Just got a report from Mallory on the freight shipments of sand on the New York Central," Herschman snapped. "Only six cars went out Tuesday afternoon on the tracks along the river up to the new bridge they're building at 168th Street; and the whole damn load was poured into the cement mixers late Tuesday night. The gun that Fennel woman threw away is cemented tight into one of the piles. Not a chance of getting it."

With a gesture of frustration he bit off the end of a cigar and spat savagely.

"If this case ever got taken up by the detective story writers," a leisurely voice from the depths of an easy-chair in a far corner remarked, "I suppose it would be called 'All Guns Missing.'"

"Oh, shut up!"

"Have it your own way, inspector."

"Got hold of Griffis yet?" Tracy asked.

"No, but I got a line on him. He's running a real estate business and he's in pretty deep. I've got Marks working on that end. He says he doesn't know yet whether there's anything crooked about his business but it looks shady. He owes a lot of money and he's keeping away from his office and his apartment. I got a good line on his history. Used to be very prosperous but in the last two years he's gone downhill."

"Well, what is our next move?" The district attorney tapped nervously with his pencil and looked at the inspector for a suggestion. But none was forthcoming. Herschman slid down on the end of his spine and puffed silently at his cigar.

"It's about time," Spike remarked, "that God gave us a break. So far we've gone ahead on our own steam. I really think we deserve a piece of good fortune, dropping unasked from the sky."

And as if in response to the hint, came Mr. Morris Shansky, not more than fifteen minutes later. At first glance Mr. Shansky's appearance was deceitful. He did not in any sense appear Heaven-sent. He was a little man, smartly gotten up with only a trace of his ancestral Yiddish accent; and as he sat in the anteroom of the district attorney's office refusing to tell his business to the secretary and insisting on a "private" interview, he was plainly nervous.

At length when his protests were of no avail, he played his trump card. Drawing Lovelace's ear down to his own level and looking about fearfully to be sure that no one might hear him, he whispered a single sentence. Even the adamantine Lovelace's stiff brows raised slightly and he disappeared into the inner office.

"A man here, Mr. Tracy," he said, "who wants to see you. He says it's about the Thane case. He insists on seeing you."

Herschman pricked up his ears, and the district attorney looked distressed. There were far too many disconcerting aspects to the case as it was, without further muddling. But with a resigned gesture he motioned the secretary to admit the visitor.

As Shansky entered the inner office he looked suspiciously at the inspector and Spike, but the district attorney cut short his protests. "This is Inspector Herschman and my brother who are assisting in the investigation. Anything you have to tell me you can tell them."

Shansky seated himself warily in the chair across the desk, not at all reassured.

"First of all, Mr. Tracy, I'm telling you," he began, "that never before in all my years in business has such a thing happened to me. Always Morris Shansky has a reputation for honor. Never has there been the slightest suspicion against my business. Always—"

"I can quite believe that, Mr. Shansky," Tracy interrupted impatiently. "What was it you wanted to tell me?"

"I'm telling you now. Ask any one on Third Avenue about me and they'll tell you that Morris Shansky deals only with respectable people. Never does he—"

"Just what is your business?"

"Pawnbroking. Licensed I am, and never have I taken anything but honest goods from honest people. Ask the cops in my district and they can tell you. Always—"

"Say lissen," Herschman broke in, "what is it you've got on your mind about the Thane case?"

Under this direct frontal attack Shansky cut short his ego-professional eulogy. In silence, he drew from an inner pocket a small box and laying it on the table pointed to it with a single word.

"That."

"Yeah, what?"

"Its—it's one of the jewels you advertised, missing from the safe of this murdered woman, Cecily Thane."

With a quick gesture Herschman reached for the box and lifted the lid. Inside, reposing on a wad of cotton, lay a diamond and emerald necklace which even to the uninitiated eye was worth a large sum of money. For a moment both the inspector, and the district attorney gasped. Then the inspector turned on Shansky, his voice tense with excitement.

"Where'd you get it?"

"I'm telling you, Mr. Inspector, always have I done an honest business. Never—"

"Lissen, brother, I know you're not a fence, so cut it. What I want to know is who brought this into your store and when and how much did you give for it?"

"A man, a small man with dark hair with a funny white streak like it was put on with a paint brush, brought it in."

"When?"

"The morning after the Thane murder—early."

"What time?"

"Early. About half past eight."

"What was his name."

"John Morgan. See, here I got the ticket."

"And how much did he want on it?"

"Five thousand dollars."

"And you gave it to him?"

"Not right away. I don't carry that much with me so early before the bank opens."

"So what did you do? Go ahead, tell it. We're not going to eat you."

"So I tell him I have to wait till nine-thirty and he says no he must have the money right away. He says his wife is going away on the boat and he must raise the money quick as she hasn't no cash with her. And I tell him, no, I got only about a thousand in the safe, will that do. So he says no, he'll come back at nine-thirty. So at nine o'clock I go to the bank and get the money and when I come back to the shop he's there again and I give it to him"

"Was he one of your regular customers?"

"No, never did I see him before. And when I read the description of the jewels in the Thane case that you send around to the licensed pawnbrokers, I know that he is the man that killed her and took them. Never has such a thing happened in my business. Always I—"

But Herschman had reached for the telephone and motioned for silence. He called the number of the Thane house, and in a few moments he had Elton Thane on the other end of the wire.

"Herschman at Headquarters, Mr. Thane. Do you know any one named John Morgan . . . No, I didn't think you did. . . . Well, do you know any one—any man with heavy dark hair with a streak of white right down the middle? What? . . . Yes. . . . Would you mind coming down here to Headquarters right away? Something very important has turned up, and we need you. . . . Yes. . . . About twenty minutes? . . . Good! . . . Say, wait a minute. Bring Emma with you. . . . Oh yes, we'll need her. All right."

Herschman hung up the receiver and turned with a triumphant smile to the district attorney. "Well, we've got—" Then he caught himself in time and nodded toward Shansky with a significant gesture.

"I'm sure, Mr. Shansky," the district attorney said, "we're greatly obliged to you for your help. It has been invaluable. Will—"

"It isn't you that needs the help, Mr. Tracy, it's me. I got my license to think of. And my five thousand dollars. How about that's?"

"My dear Mr. Shansky, if there are any difficulties about the renewal of your license, please communicate with me and I will give the matter my personal attention. And as for the five thousand dollars, you are fully protected by the insurance on the jewels which will cover your loss. In the meantime won't you step outside and let my secretary have your name and address and telephone number in case we want to get in touch with you?"

With a firm and final gesture Herschman himself personally escorted Shansky into the waiting room before he had an opportunity to enter any further defense of his impeccable reputation. He could hardly wait to close the door on the pawnbroker's back.

"Thane says," he explained, his voice shaking with excitement, "that the only man he knows with bushy black hair with a white streak down the middle is Mrs. Thane's brother, George Griffis."

In the half hour which it took Elton Thane to drive from Eighty-second Street to Police Headquarters, Herschman was busy investigating the pawnbroker. He found that Shansky's record was all that Shansky had claimed.

Thane arrived, breathless and puzzled and left Emma in the anteroom while he went into the district attorney's office. The two days which had elapsed since they had last seen him had wrought a decided change in his appearance. The weariness and pain had disappeared from his face and there was a quiet sense of calm about him.

Herschman could hardly wait for the preliminary greetings to be finished.

"There, Mr. Thane," and he pointed triumphantly to the little pasteboard box in which the glittering jewels lay.

Thane's eyes went wide as he gazed at it. "The necklace! But how—"

"A pawnbroker brought it in this morning," Herschman explained. "Not a fence. We looked him up. A licensed pawnbroker."

"But where did he get it? Did Spencer—"

"No, not Spencer. A man who gave the name of John Morgan, a man with bushy black hair with a streak of white down the center."

"George!"

Herschman nodded. For a moment Thane was stunned. Then he broke out. "It—it can't be. He's her own brother. He—he lived in the house with us."

"Exactly! And even when he moved out he kept his latchkey."

"Are you sure, Mr. Thane," the district attorney broke in, "that you have told us all you know about Griffis' visit to your wife the afternoon before she was—last Monday afternoon?"

"Yes, everything. I saw her for only a moment, you know, before she went out with Spencer and all she said was, 'George was here this afternoon.'"

"I think we had better have the maid in," Tracy suggested, and nodded to Herschman. In a few moments Emma Bloomstead entered the room. She hesitated at the threshold and looked uneasily, at the three men before her. Then her glance traveled to Thane as if in silent question. But he spoke with gentle reassurance.

"The gentlemen here, Emma, have a few questions they would like to ask you."

She said nothing as she took the chair which Spike pulled up for her.

"Emma," said the district attorney going straight to the point, "Mr. Thane tells us that on last Monday afternoon, Mrs. Thane's brother, George Griffis visited her."

"Yes, sir."

"At what time did he come?"

"Oh, some time in the afternoon. About four I guess. I don't know exactly."

"Didn't you let him in?"

"No, sir. He used his key he used to have when he was living there."

"Did you see him when he went out or at any time while he was in the house?"

"No, sir."

"Then how do you know that he came to the house?"

"I heard his voice."

"Suppose you tell us about it."

"I was going up to my room from the basement to get a clean apron and I had to pass right by the door of Mrs. Thane's sitting room."

"The door was open?"

"No, it was closed tight."

"But you could hear the voices?"

"Yes, they were talking loud."

"Did you stop and listen?"

"Well—yes." Emma admitted her eavesdropping with a proper lowering of the eyes. "I couldn't hear Mrs. Thane. She was talking low and natural, I guess, but Mr. Griffis was talking very loud."

"And could you hear what he was saying?"

"Well—some." It was plain that she was loath to make the admission.

"And what did you hear?"

Again her eyes sought Thane's.

"Go on, Emma, tell them whatever you heard." His voice was quiet but there was a certain tenseness about his jaw as he spoke

"I—I couldn't make out all of it very well, but he kept saying something about the bank and $5,000."

The district attorney and Herschman exchanged significant glances.

"All right, go on"

"And then he'd say, 'I've got to have it I tell you,' and Mrs. Thane would say something low so I couldn't hear and finally he said something about—" She stopped and this time as she looked at Elton Thane there was positive fright in her eyes. "Then he said something about Mr. Thane."

"What?"

"He said, 'By —by Jesus, if I told all I know about that lousy husband of yours, you wouldn't dare be so damn stingy.'"

She stopped again, toying nervously with the edge of her purse, and again the district attorney pushed her on with the story.

"And what else did he say?"

"I didn't hear any more. The telephone rang just then and I had to go back down into the front hall to answer it. It was a call for the cook and I had to go downstairs to get her, and I stopped in the kitchen for a few minutes while she was gone to tend some stuff she had on the stove. And a little while later when I went upstairs the door was open to Mrs. Thane's room, and she called me in to tell me something about dinner, and he was gone."

There was a stiff, tense silence as Emma brought her story to a close.

"And you are sure that is all you overheard?"

"Yes, sir."

Tracy motioned her to withdraw and when she had left the room, both the district attorney and Herschman with one accord fastened their eyes on Elton Thane.

"Tell me, Mr. Thane," Tracy said, "have you any idea to what Mr. Griffis referred by the remark which your maid has just repeated?"

"I'm sure I can't imagine what he was talking about."

"You know of no financial difficulties of your brother-in-law?"

"As a matter of fact, I understand he hasn't been doing well lately, but I have no direct knowledge of his affairs."

"Can you explain in any way his reference to you?"

"George and I have never—well, we have never been on particularly good terms with each other."

"And yet he lived in your house until a year ago?"

"Yes."

"What was the nature of your difficulty with him?"

"Oh, just a difference in temperament. In-laws, you know, are not notoriously good friends."

"And you are quite sure that you don't know what he meant when he said, 'If I told all I know about that lousy husband of yours you wouldn't dare—?'"

Tracy paused and looked directly at Thane. Slowly Thane's eyes dropped.

"Mr. Tracy, I think perhaps I had better be honest with you," he said in a voice that was barely audible.

"So you do know?"

"Yes Three years ago I—I was up against the wall. Things had been on the upgrade for me, and then I lost heavily in the market. I had to have $50,000 or I would have lost $500,000. So I—I—I—signed my brother-in-law's name to a check."

No one spoke and for a moment Elton Thane let this simple and damning confession stand unqualified. Then quickly he went on in a louder, surer tone. "But I paid him back, every cent—later when I made money. Every cent and eight per cent interest."

"In cash?"

"Yes, he wouldn't take a check."

"Did your wife know of this forgery?"

"Yes, she knew. She—she got the check afterward and kept it."

"You mean to say, Mr. Thane," Herschman put in in a slightly incredulous manner, "that your wife held a check which you had forged for $50,000?"

Thane nodded.

"How did she get it and where did she keep it?"

"She persuaded George to give it to her—and, and I never did know where she kept it."

"Then how did you know she had it, still?"

"She—she used to remind me of it."

"Remind you of it? In what way?"

"Good God, man," Thane suddenly gave way.

It was as if the muscles which had been holding him calm and erect had melted within him. His shoulder slumped helplessly and his voice came hoarse and broken.

"God! Can't you understand that for three years she's held that check over my head—me—her own husband—and after she persuaded me to do it. I didn't want to. I swear I didn't. She made me.

"We went to George and asked him for the money and he refused. And I had to have $50,000 or my whole business, everything I had would go. So she made me do it. She said she'd keep George from prosecuting. She did—she kept him from prosecuting. But she got the check herself and she's held it over my head ever since She's—Oh, my God!"

With a sudden movement of despair Elton Thane Hung his head forward in his hands and choked back the torrent of words that came from his tortured lips.

XI. Elton Thane in a Tight Place

FOR a moment there was a tense silence in the room, broken only by a sudden intake of breath from the bowed figure opposite the district attorney.

"Are you quite sure," the district attorney said at last in a very quiet voice, "that you realize what you are saying?"

Thane lifted a haggard, drawn face to the prosecutor. He seemed to have aged at least ten years in the last ten minutes. He nodded his head dumbly.

"Yes, I know what I'm saying—and I know what you're thinking. But I didn't! I swear to God I didn't." His voice rose hoarse and shrill.

"No one is jumping at conclusions, Mr. Thane, but under the circumstances I shall have to ask you to give us a very careful outline of your actions last Monday night."

Thane made an effort to pull himself together and ran his tongue over his dry lips. But when he spoke his voice was once more under control.

"All right. Go ahead. Ask me whatever you want to."

"Suppose you go ahead."

"I left the house about eight or half past, I don't know just when, and went to my club, the Chatham on Seventy-second Street, and stayed there almost all evening."

"Do you remember the names of any of the people who saw you there? Did you talk to any one?"

"Yes. About ten o'clock I got in a bridge game with J. P. Crandall and Horace Pullman and another fellow. I forget his name. Some friend of Crandall's."

"And how long did you stay there?"

"Till almost twelve. And then I remembered that I'd promised Dr. Partridge next door—you met him that first morning—I'd promised him I'd drop into his place for some chess. So I left the club and went to his house."

"You walked?"

"Yes."

"And you went directly without stopping off any place?"

"Yes."

"And you—"

"No. Wait a minute. I did stop at a cigar store. The one at the corner of Columbus and Seventy-sixth Street and got a couple of packages of cigarettes and some cigars. I'd promised Partridge to come much earlier in the evening, and I'd gotten so engrossed in the bridge game that I'd partly forgotten about my promise. So I thought I'd take some of his favorite cigars as a sort of peace offering."

"And that was the only place you stopped?"

"You went right from the cigar store to Dr. Partridge's house?" The eyes of Herschman seemed boring into Elton Thane, but they failed of their effect. Thane seemed to divine what was in the inspector's mind.

"No," he said, "I didn't go into my own house. I went directly to Dr. Partridge's."

"At what time did you arrive at Dr. Partridge's?"

"Oh, somewhere around twelve."

"That's pretty indefinite."

"I know, but it's the best I can do."

"And you stayed at Dr. Partridge's until when?"

"About four."

"All the time?"

"All the time."

Herschman's brows came together in a calculating line and he looked quizzically at Thane.

"I tell you what, Mr. Thane, I'm going to ask you to stay here for a little while. In there," and the inspector indicated a door at the far end of the office. Thane acquiesced without protest and followed him through the door, and down a long hall to a small office, where two patrolmen were playing cards.

"Don't let this gentleman here disturb you, boys," he said as he motioned Thane to a chair. "He's just waiting here a little while for me."

One of the men looked up from his cards and nodded with an almost imperceptible lift of his eyebrows

Herschman hurried back to the district attorney's office and grabbed the telephone. "Get me the house of Dr. Partridge on West Eighty-second Street." While he was waiting for the number he explained to Tracy. "I'm going to get Partridge down here double-quick and check on that story. I've left Matt and Parker with Thane."

In a few moments the connection was through and the high-pitched but pompous voice of Dr. Partridge himself answered. He would be delighted to put himself at the service of the police department One gathered from his tone that be felt that he had been rather neglected of late, and was only too glad to step once more into the limelight.

In the brief time which elapsed between the call and Partridge's arrival at Headquarters, Herschman dispatched a detective to the cigar store at the corner of Columbus and Seventy-sixth Street in search of the clerk who had been on duty the previous Monday night.

Dr. Partridge smiled genially as he entered the office. Removed by three miles and the lapse of three days from the night of his neighbor's tragedy, he seemed more naturally himself, much less impressive and ridiculously pompous.

"I'm sorry to trouble you, Dr. Partridge," the district attorney explained, "but there are certain points in connection with the Thane case which are not, as yet, quite clear in our minds. So I'm going to ask you to go over a few of them with us."

Partridge nodded in compliance and seated himself in the chair which had so recently been vacated by Thane.

"How long have you known the Thanes?"

The meticulous little man thought for a moment and then gave his precise answer. "It will be four years next month that the Thanes moved into the house next to mine. About five months later Mr. Thane called me in a hurry one night about half past twelve. His wife had been taken ill suddenly, and although I have been retired from active practice for the last ten years, in an emergency I answer calls. The case was a simple one—indigestion and hysteria, but mostly hysteria. My acquaintance with Mr. Thane dates from that night."

"Was Mrs. Thane subject to such attacks frequently?"

"Well, yes, occasionally. She was rather a highly strung woman, and, if I may say so, given to violent fits of temper, which usually ended up in an attack."

"And so you treated her off and on for these attacks of hysteria?"

"Yes, though it would hardly be called treatment. I merely administered a sedative which is all those cases usually demand."

"What in your opinion brought on these attacks?"

"Temper! Pure temper!" Dr. Partridge's small, precise little mouth under its drooping walrus mustache pulled itself down into a decided disapproving line.

"Temper brought on by a quarrel with her husband?" Tracy suggested.

The doctor nodded reluctantly.

"What did they usually quarrel about?"

"I do not inquire into the private lives of my patients, unless they ask me to do so."

"But surely, Doctor, you came to know the Thanes very well, and you could not help but understand any difficulties that may have arisen between them."

"No, I knew only Mr. Thane. I never saw Mrs. Thane except when I was called in professionally. But early in my acquaintance with Mr. Thane we discovered a mutual fondness for chess, and as I have already told you, we often played quite far into the night."

"How often were you in the habit of playing chess with Mr. Thane?"

"At least once a week, but lately twice and sometimes three times."

"How late do you usually play?"

"Sometimes until half past one or two."

"But last Monday night you played until four?"

"Yes. That is the latest that we have ever kept at it."

"Didn't you get very sleepy?"

"Yes, but Thane was having a run of bad luck and he was trying to recoup his losses. We always play for a small stake, you understand. A purely nominal sum, just enough to add a slight zest to the game. Under the circumstances, I could hardly suggest quitting."

"In what part of your house were you playing, Doctor?"

"In the front parlor on the first floor."

"You and Mr. Thane were in that room all the time until four o'clock when he left—both of you?"

"Both of us—all the time," the doctor declared emphatically. Then quickly he corrected himself. "No. Wait. Once Thane left the room, but just out into the hall to the front door. It was a fairly warm night and we both of us laid off our coats and vests, but even then it was not comfortable, so he stepped out into the hall and opened the front door."

"And how long was he gone from the room?"

"Twenty seconds, perhaps half a minute."

"And that was the only time that either one of you was out of the room?"

"Well, now that I think back, I left the room a little bit later to go down to the basement to fetch a decanter of wine."

"And how long were you gone?"

"I couldn't have been more than a minute. The stairs are just outside the door of the parlor, and the bottle was in the cupboard directly at the foot of the stairs. I had only to run down and back again."

"Now tell me, Doctor," Herschman broke in, "at what time did Mr. Thane arrive at your house last Monday night?"

The doctor thought for a moment, in an earnest effort at accuracy. "It was exactly ten minutes of twelve."

"Why do you say exactly?"

"I say exactly because that is exactly what time it was. Ten minutes of twelve."

"Do you usually remember time so accurately?"

"No," he admitted frankly. "I don't. But in this particular case I do. When I had seen Mr. Thane earlier in the day and he had suggested a round of chess that night, he said he would be over at eleven-thirty. I am a person who keeps appointments promptly, and I expect the same promptness in others. When he did not arrive at eleven-thirty, I grew impatient. When he did come finally, I drew my watch out, to reproach him and I showed it to him. He was twenty minutes late. It was exactly ten minutes of twelve. Of that I am positive."

"Did he bring you anything as a sort of peace offering?"

The little doctor suddenly smiled. "Indeed he did. He brought me five boxes of my favorite cigars."

"Five boxes?"

"Five boxes!"

"And you're quite sure about the time of Thane's arrival at your house?"

"Quite sure. There can be no mistake about that."

Herschman's expression was one of disgruntled defeat. When the door had closed on the doctor, he slumped down into a chair and looked ruefully at the district attorney.

"Well, another good theory all shot to hell. That is, if that little bird is telling the truth and I think he is." For some quite inexplicable reason which even he himself could not have analyzed, the inspector looked not to the district attorney but to Spike for confirmation.

"Yes, Inspector, I think you're right. Too bad isn't it. I'm all cut up. It would have made such a nice story for the tabs—'Slayer Plays Chess, After Shooting Wife.'"

"I think I'll ask that maid just once more when Spencer left the house," Herschman said with sudden decision. "See if she tells the same story twice."

But when Emma was once more before the three men, she only reaffirmed her original emphasis on the precise time of Spencer's departure

"Yes, sir. I'm sure it was almost exactly twelve. Or maybe just a minute or so after. I looked at the clock especially."

XII. The Gigolo Racket

THE report of the detective whom Herschman had sent to the cigar store on Seventy-second Street and Columbus Avenue only lent further credence to Thane's story. The clerk in question remembered distinctly his customer of the previous Monday night.

"Sure I remember him," he replied to the detective's question "He bought five boxes of the most expensive cigars we carry. He wanted six, but we only had five in stock, so he took all we had."

"And what time was he in the store?" the detective asked.

"A little before twelve, about ten or fifteen minutes before. I noticed particularly because I close up at twelve and along about the last half hour, I keep a pretty close watch on the clock. Yeah, just about fifteen, twenty minutes to twelve, I'd say."

When the detective brought this information bark to Headquarters, Herschman merely grunted and relayed it to the district attorney's office.

"What I want to know," Herschman said, "is where are we headed for next? This case is getting too damn complicated."

"I should think a nice quiet little talk with George Griffis would be interesting," Spike suggested.

"Yeah." The word was heavy with sarcasm.

"Well, if you two can possibly do without my company for a little while I think I'll go up and chin a bit with Tommy."

As neither the district attorney nor the inspector paid any attention to his suggestion, Spike took their indifference for consent, left Headquarters and crossed the street to the Tombs. On his way he stopped and bought a bag of fruit, a carton of cigarettes, two hot dogs and the latest edition of the *Graphic*.

The story which it carried of the Thane case bore obvious evidence of a city editor's insistent demands for new and exciting developments when nothing new was forthcoming from the official source of information. Tommy Spencer was the chief preoccupation of reportorial ingenuity. From the morgue there had been dug up old pictures when he went more accurately by the name of William Preston and was just starting out in business as the dancing partner of Mrs. Greta Schlockenhass.

From Murray there was an account of Spencer's movements on Monday night. Quickly Spike scanned the type for the name of Nina Fennel or, at least for some reference to a "mystery woman." Knowing the tabloid penchant for mystery women, he did not trust even the chivalrous discretion of Murray under the unscrupulous onslaughts of wiley reporters. But apparently he had misjudged the butler. There was no reference to Spencer's feminine visitor on the momentous night of the tragedy.

At the jail he was readily admitted, his relationship with the district attorney proving an open sesame to the most heavily barred door. He found Spencer slumped disconsolately on the hard iron cot which was the only furniture which the cell afforded.

"Really," said Spike reprovingly, "you offend me, Tommy. Positively offend me, you're that gloomy. Here, lighten your soul, if not your stomach with a hot dog," and he sat cross-legged on the floor and opened his purchases.

"You're a hell of a one to talk to me about being gloomy," Tommy grumbled, and bit savagely into a hot frankfurter.

"It is rather nervy of me, isn't it," Spike replied complacently. "Me with the freedom of the city, and you shut up in this bloody cell."

Tommy looked at his visitor uneasily. Yet at the same time it was plain that he welcomed company after the monotony of solitude. His obvious impulse to talk was warring with a certain wariness which was only half concealed.

"Anything new?" he asked.

"Just chatting with Mr. Thane."

"Yes, that's the best thing he does."

"Oh, really? He always impressed me as being frightfully reticent."

"Thane? Why, he's one of the gabbiest fellows I know. I never once went to call for Mrs. Thane but what he was sticking around entertaining me in the parlor before she came, just like he was her little brother and I was her boyfriend."

"Well, you were, weren't you?"

Tommy shook his head. "No, it was strictly business between Mrs. Thane and me. She paid prompt—or fairly prompt, and I gave good service, and that was that."

"Tommy, you're shockingly commercial."

"The more 'commercial' you are the better you get on in my line."

"What sort of a person was she, anyway? You know we have surprisingly little information about the woman herself."

"Oh, she was all right."

"Meaning nothing at all. Be a bit more specific."

"Oh, well, she was the sort most of my customers are. Tired of their husbands, wanting some one they can't get, and nothing to fill up their time. Some of them get nervous breakdowns and call in a doctor to send them to Bermuda. And some of them call in me to take them to a nightclub."

"Incidentally, how does one go about working up a—ah—a clientele such as yours?"

"Oh, different ways. Usually if you're seen around a lot at a night club some woman will spot you and get a line on you. Sometimes you get called in to take extra women around—you know, when Cousin Susie arrives unexpectedly from Dubuque and there isn't a man for her. Sometimes the woman's husband even hires you. That's the way I got roped in on that Schlockenhass case. The old boy liked to sit around in his stocking feet with his bucket of beer and a corn cob, and his wife wanted something a little bit livelier, so he got me to keep her busy so he could have time nights to read his *Police Gazette* in comfort."

"Tommy, let me ask you just once more about that Schlockenhass case. Are you quite sure you've been truthful about it?"

"Honest to God, I'm telling you the truth. I didn't have any more to do with killing Mrs. Schlockenhass than I did with killing Mrs. Thane. It was just my damn luck, though, to be with each woman before the fellow that did the job came along."

"What makes you so sure that it was a 'fellow?'" Spike posed the question casually through a leisurely cloud of cigarette smoke.

"Sure it was a man," Tommy shot back quickly. "Women haven't the nerve for that sort of thing. Anyway, what woman would have it in for Mrs. Thane?"

"Well, for that matter, what man?"

"How should I know? I'm not the dick in this case I'm just the goat."

"You know," Spike confessed with a smile of amusement, "this situation despite its tragic ending, intrigues me no end. I mean your calling at the house for the wife and the husband entertaining you until she got ready. Sounds like something out of a Lonsdale comedy drama. Just what sort of thing does one talk about under the circumstances?"

"Oh, I dunno. Almost anything. What you read in the newspapers, or the weather or golf—Thane's a golf bug— (Took me with him once or twice, but I never could get much interested in it)—where you're going that night. He was always particular where I took Mrs. Thane. If she'd been eighteen and he was her mother, he couldn't have been any fussier about knowing that we were going places that he considered respectable, and what time we were getting home and all that."

"I suppose you hear lots of interesting stories from your—ah—clients?"

"What do you mean, interesting stories?"

"I mean most of your clients confess that their husbands 'don't understand them.'"

"Yes, that's their line. But I will say this for Mrs. Thane. She never pulled that one on me. She never talked about her troubles."

"Oh, so she did have some—troubles?"

"No woman hires a man to take her around to night clubs unless she's got something bearing down on her chest."

"And Cecily Thane never got hers off her chest?"

"Not to me."

"Just a straight business proposition."

"Strictly business, that's me."

"Frightfully embarrassing, though, I should think."

"Embarrassing? Why?"

"I mean the financial end. Did you submit a monthly bill or was it a pay-as-you-enter proposition?"

"At the beginning of each evening she'd give me $100. That was expenses and my rake-off."

"You never had any—ah—arguments with Mrs. Thane about money?"

"No, not arguments. Once or twice she didn't have the cash and she asked me to stand her till the next time and she'd pay double. Thane, you know, is as stingy as hell."

"Really?"

"Yes. Once when we drove out to his golf club the bill was $5 and he gave the taxi driver a quarter. Can you tie that?"

"And yet," Spike persisted, "you're quite sure that there were never any money troubles between you and Mrs. Thane?"

"Sure. I'm telling you."

"I know, Tommy, old thing, but under the circumstances do you mind if I'm rather skeptical?"

But Tommy only grunted and spat out a seed.

"By the way," Spike went on, "how did you happen to acquire Mrs. Thane's patronage?"

"A girl I know introduced me to her. Dame named Audrey Keating. She's a show girl and every once in a while she steers me on to something good."

"I didn't know Mrs. Thane had many friends in the profession. How did Miss Keating happen to know her?"

"She never said. I just met her down at the Lido Club one night after the show and she said she had a job for me, and the next night she brought Mrs. Thane to the club and we've been doing business from then on."

"Tell me, did Mrs. Thane ever—was shea— Well, what I'm trying to say, is—was she in love with you?"

"Say, listen I'm telling you that I'm running a business. And I use business methods. All she wanted was some one to go out and dance with her."

"Something you said a moment ago, intrigued me," Spike went on. "You said that most of your customers were women who were tired of their husbands, 'wanting some one they couldn't get.' Just who was it that Mrs. Thane wanted that she couldn't get?"

"How should I know?" Tommy bit quickly into a pear and filled his mouth with an overlarge bite.

"Oh, I just thought you might have a hint of it," Spike said nonchalantly and let the matter rest. "Interesting profession, yours. How ever did you come to select it?"

"I didn't select it. I started doing it because I was broke and down on my luck, and I found out the only thing I could do to make money was to dance. I wasn't good enough for stage dancing, but I could get by on the gigolo racket."

"You're not a native New Yorker I take it from your accent."

"No, I came from a little town out in the Middle West. You'd never think it, but I clerked in a grocery store. And then I came to the great city to make good as a popular song writer." Tommy paused as an expression, half wistful, half cynical crept into his eyes. "Poor goof! I didn't know until after I got here that song writing was a closed corporation, and I had about as much chance of breaking into it as I would breaking into grand opera. I got flatter and flatter, and finally just when I was down to my last five, I met up with a guy that put me next to this business. I've been at it ever since, almost two years. And I wish to hell I'd never set eyes on a night club or a jazz band."

"There's somethmg about the way you say all this, Tommy that makes me feel that your heart is not in your work."

"You're damn right it isn't."

"But really it seems to me that $100 a night is shockingly good pay, and for dancing with beautiful women."

"Beautiful women! God, if you could see some of the freaks that I've taken out. But that's not the worst of it. There's something about the business of being a professional dancing man, that when you meet a real girl—I mean a girl that really matters—why she sort of looks down—she thinks you're nothing but a—" Tommy stumbled hopelessly and Spike tactfully came to the rescue.

"I quite understand" He rose and stretched himself after his cramped position on the floor, and gathered up his hat and stick from the end of the cot. In the doorway of the cell he paused.

"I might be going up to see Nina Fennel," he said and smiled. "Any message you'd like to give her?"

For a moment Spencer only stared at him. Then he too smiled a little ruefully. "That's right, kick a guy when he's down. I suppose you're going to cop off the only real dame I ever knew, while I'm shut up in this goddam jail."

"Oh, no, Tommy, you mistake me. Much as I would like to do so, I wouldn't be permitted to go alone. I would be amply chaperoned by my brother and Inspector Herschman."

Out of the corner of his eye as be turned and walked down the corridor, Spike could see Spencer's knuckles go white as he gripped the edge of his cot and stared straight before him with frightened eyes.

XIII. George Griffis in a Tight Place

AT eleven o'clock on the fourth morning after the murder of Cecily Thane, Inspector Herschman and District Attorney Tracy retired from their morning round with the newspaper men, after hinting that a complete denouement might be expected at any moment.

But when they closed the door on the last of the reporters they relapsed into a state of pessimism which was sharply in contrast to their attitude before their recent questioners. Spike, who during the week had assumed almost the aspect of a permanent fixture in his brother's office, was as usual sprawled in an easy-chair, smoking and regarding his two companions with a slight smile of amusement. Neither Herschman nor Tracy was in a talkative mood and the room was steeped in a gloomy silence.

"Well," said Spike at length, "since there doesn't seem anything else which demands our immediate attention, let's talk about the murder of Cecily Thane."

Herschman gave him a dark look and Tracy's mouth set itself in the disapproving line which his brother's carefree attitude usually evoked.

"As things stand now," Spike went on disregarding the frosty reception which his suggestion had received, "we have a most interesting array of people who were in or about the Thane premises on the fatal night of May 15. There is, for instance, Tommy Spencer. Tommy has already been involved in a similar case, he's hard up for money, and he quite definitely told his valet that he expected to 'raise quite a large sum soon'.

"And then there's George Griffis, estranged brother, who hocked a necklace known to have been in the dead woman's possession. . .

"And then there's Elton Thane himself, whose best friend and severest critic has for the last three years been making him toe the mark by threatening him with a check which he forged.

"Not to mention Emma the maid. On the occasion of our first conversation with her, Emma talked like one whose life is an open book and who joys in the confessing. But ever since then she has acted like a scared bunny.

"In sharp contrast to Emma's two-timing tactics is Dr. Peregrine Partridge who, I have a feeling, is one of the few persons involved who is telling God's truth and nothing else but."

Spike paused a moment. "And then there is Nina Fennel," he pointed out quietly.

"Yeah, that's what I say," Herschman snapped. "If I had my way about this I'd go up there and strong arm that dame."

"But, my dear inspector, you must realize that Miss Fennel is definitely not the type that one strong arms. I have a feeling that it is best to let matters stand just as they are with her for the present. For no reason at all I don't believe the time is ripe to call her attention to the fact that she lied like a lady.

"I don't believe that the letter which Cecily Thane wrote Mrs. Fennel was merely a kindly inquiry about her health, any more than I believe that Miss Fennel and her father dropped in on the Thanes Monday night for 'just a friendly chat'. And it looks very much like Miss Fennel and Tommy have a little secret between themselves that they're not telling us. Furthermore, throwing guns into sand cars is not precisely the sort of thing one does when one's conscience is carefree and spotless."

"I'll say it isn't," Herschman said

"But the thing that puzzles me is the delay. It seems to me if I had just shot some one and was going to dispose of my gun, I'd pick the first garbage can I struck."

"Say, lissen, brother," Herschman gave some patronizing advice, "when you've been dealing with crooks as long as I have, you'll learn that even the smartest of them do the damndest fool things."

"I suppose it was only from the naiveté of my own ignorance, Inspector, that I brought forth the quaint idea."

Herschman eyed Spike uneasily. Words like "naiveté" and "quaint" were not in his vocabulary and they annoyed him.

"Well, now you've got 'em lined up," he grumbled, "what are you going to do with them? Spencer, Griffis, Thane and the Fennel girl. Thane's got an alibi. He arrived at Partridge's at ten of twelve and his wife wasn't killed until after twelve."

"Unless," Spike reminded him, "Tommy did it."

The inspector nodded in agreement. "But there's some one you're forgetting, aren't you?" the district attorney broke in.

"Who?"

"Mortimer Fennel."

"Well," said Spike, "the inspector may have forgotten him, but not I. As a matter of fact, I find him most intriguing."

"But we haven't got anything on him like we have on the daughter," Herschman countered.

"No," Spike admitted. "Nothing except the fact that he was seen entering the Thane house Monday night. But no one saw him leave. And, what is still more important, unless I'm very much mistaken, he seems to be the object of a good deal of concern on the part of his daughter. I have a feeling that she much prefers having us talk to her, than to her father."

"You mean—" But whatever the inspector was about to ask was interrupted by the ringing of the telephone. With the nervous eagerness of one under a tension he grabbed it, before the district attorney had an opportunity to reach for it.

It was a summons for him to come to his own office down the corridor. He left the room but in less than five minutes he was back, an excited light in his eyes and a triumphant smile turning up the corners of his mouth.

"They've got Griffis."

Both Spike and the district attorney sat forward in their chairs.

"Got him! McCauley's just telephoned that he's bringing him over here. Got him through his bank. Got a line on him from a real estate company he was trading with and found that he did business with the Corn Exchange branch at Fourth Avenue and Twenty-ninth Street. McCauley buttonholes the president and finds out that on Tuesday morning Griffis appeared at the bank and met a $5,000 note that they held on him. But he had another note for $2,000 that came, due today. McCauley stuck around and sure enough Griffis turns up and renews it. As he walks out McCauley grabs him."

Fifteen minutes later Detective McCauley walked in with his prisoner. George Griffis was a young man, perhaps thirty-four or five with a pale pasty face that seemed prematurely etched with lines, from which peered apprehensive blue eyes. Although of average height, he somehow gave the impression of being a small man. Perhaps it was his sloping shoulders, perhaps the uneasy way he carried his head ducked forward slightly.

As he stood now before the inspector and the district attorney, his eyes jumped nervously and his bony fingers played with the side flaps of his pockets. A thin, negative fellow that you would have passed a hundred times without seeing, had it not been for the strange marking of his hair.

Heavy and bushy and black. You wondered where such an anemic, ineffectual creature had gotten the strength to grow, much less support such a vigorous healthy mop. And straight through the center, as if it had been put on with a paint brush, ran a streak of pure white.

He seated himself nervously in the chair which the district attorney indicated. At a sign from the inspector, McCauley withdrew.

"You are aware Mr. Griffis," the district attorney began, "why you are here?"

"Y—yes." For the first time he spoke and his voice trembled and broke even on the one word.

"Then just why," Herschman broke in, "have you been hiding out on us?"

"I—I haven't been hiding."

"Where have you been the last three days?"

"I had to go out of town on business."

"What business?"

"I'm in the real estate business and I had to see a man down in Camden about some property I have my eye on."

"His name?"

"Pearsall. He's with Jones & Pearsall. They're a firm I do business with often."

"And that's the one and only reason you've not been in New York since Tuesday morning."

"Yes, sir."

"Ever see this before?"

Herschman tossed Cecily Thane's diamond and emerald necklace down on the desk before Griffis with a careless gesture as if it were so much glass. Griffis swallowed and his eyes bulged slightly.

"Yes. It—it belonged to my sister. She gave it to me." He seemed to rush the words out.

"She *gave* it to you?"

"Yes, Monday afternoon, just the day before she was murdered."

Herschman, who had been pacing the floor in front of his victim, slowly settled himself into a chair and carefully folded his arms and let his half-closed eyes rest on Griffis.

"Suppose you tell us about it." His voice was quiet but steel edged.

"Well—I went to see her Monday afternoon, and I was rather pressed for money, and I asked her for some. She said she didn't have any, and she'd been spending so much lately that she hated to ask her husband for any more. He's rather close, you know. And so she said she'd let me have that, and I could raise some money on it temporarily. I've got some more coming in next month, you understand, so I could easily redeem it and I was going to give it back to her then."

"I see," said Herschman and a slightly ironic smile twisted up the corner of his mouth "Did you go to see your sister often?"

"Well—fairly often—"

"I suppose, of course, you were pretty fond of your sister. Her death makes you feel pretty terrible."

"Well, yes, naturally"

"On Monday afternoon when you saw her did she seem—worried about anything or upset?"

"No more than usual"

"What do you mean, no more than usual?"

"Well, she was always a nervous, excitable sort of person."

"And was she nervous and excited when you saw her?"

"Oh, she was just about as usual."

"How long did you stay?"

"About twenty or thirty minutes."

"Just a nice little brother and sister visit. You told her about your money difficulties and she promised to help you out and gave you her necklace."

"Yes."

"Just kind and helpful and sisterly."

"Yes."

Herschman paused. Then he shot the next question so suddenly that Griffis started visibly in his chair.

"Did Thane ever pay you back the $50,000 for the check he forged on you?"

"—Uh—no."

"Never paid you a cent?"

"No."

"Why didn't you prosecute?"

"On account of my sister."

"Where's the check now?"

"I don't know. Cecily made me give it to her very soon after it happened and I've never seen it since."

"I suppose she took it from you to make sure that you would never use it?"

"Yes, she wanted to protect her husband."

"Why did you move away from the Thane house last year?"

"Why—uh—I had a fight with Ce—with Thane."

"What about?"

"I was trying to make him pay back the money he forged on me."

"And did he do it?"

"No. I told you before."

"You didn't have a fight with your sister"

"No. We were always—very good friends." Again Herschman paused, and in the interim Spike spoke from his corner in the easy-chair.

"By the way, Mr. Griffis, did you by any chance notice whether your sister was writing a letter when you came in?"

"No."

"And I don't suppose you know whether she happened to be acquainted with any one by the name of Fennel?"

The muscles around Griffis' thin mouth seemed to tighten.

"Well—yes—she did."

"Very well?"

"Oh, no," he said quickly. "Mor—Mr. Fennel—the Fennels—" He floundered. "The Fennels used to live next door to them when they were on Eighty-sixth Street."

"And have they kept up the friendship since then— since the Thanes moved away?"

"No, they've hardly seen anything of them." Again the quick negative.

"Your witness, Inspector," and Spike lapsed once more into the indolence of smoking.

A sardonic smile twisted Herschman's face. He surveyed Griffis in much the same manner as a cat looks at a mouse with which it is playing in its quiet, torturing fashion. Griffis pulled out his handkerchief and wiped the beaded moisture from his forehead.

"What," said Herschman with a misleading leisureliness, "what was the situation between your sister and her husband—friendly?"

For a moment Griffis' nervous hands stopped fiddling with the edge of his coat. For the flash of a second a sudden alert gleam seemed to light his eye. When he spoke again his voice was more controlled than at any time during the meeting.

"They were not," he said carefully as if choosing his words; "they were not very well fitted."

"How do you mean?"

"I mean my sister, like any woman, did not enjoy being neglected by her husband."

"He neglected her?"

"Yes. She was a very lonely woman." Griffis' voice became low, shot through with a certain note of suffering.

"I suppose there were other women?"

"I can't say whether there were 'women.' But there was a woman."

"Yes?"

"Elton Thane has been running around with a show girl for the past year, and my sister was almost beside herself."

"Did Thane ever speak to your sister about a divorce?"

"Many times He begged her to divorce him."

"And she wouldn't do it?"

"Certainly not. She—she loved him." The note of pain increased.

"You know who this woman is?"

"She was in some revue, but I understand she isn't working now." The last part of the sentence was uttered with a certain quietness that spoke far more than the actual words.

"Know where she lives?"

"No."

"Name?"

"I only know her first name. It's Audrey."

Herschman reached for the telephone and got his own office on the wire. "McCauley," he said when the connection had been put through, "get all the programs of Broadway revues for the last year and locate any girls in them named Audrey. And bring 'em around to my office."

XIV: Miss Keating Forgets to be Dramatic

ONCE more the papers buzzed with the news of an arrest in the Thane murder case—George Griffis, brother of the murdered woman. His picture three columns wide and beneath it a photograph of the necklace which had been turned over to the police by the impeccably honest Shansky Even Shansky came in for his share of the publicity posed in front of his Third Avenue three-balled shop.

And once more Spike glanced over the headlines as he rode north in a taxicab to an address on East Ninety-third Street—an address which he had only five minutes before obtained from Tommy Spencer in his cell in the Tombs. The number, a few doors east of Madison Avenue, proved to be an apartment house of the obviously swanky sort, with a uniformed doorman, and a telephone operator in the hall who discreetly took your name and relayed it to the apartment before permitting you to be shot up in the elevator.

The door of Miss Audrey Keating's apartment was opened by a black and white starched French maid who looked as if she might have dropped out of a moving picture. Indeed, the entire interior was not unlike the more luxurious Hollywood sets of ladies of easy but shrewd virtue. It was obvious that Miss Keating was all that is popularly expected of a lady of the chorus who plays with millionaires in her off hours.

Nor did Miss Keating herself differ greatly from the popular conception. She appeared in a luxurious scarlet dressing gown whose sleek, clinging folds revealed those melting lines which were her fortune. A tall, striking, blonde with that particular brand of eyes which are never known as merely blue, but baby blue. Yet with it all, there was a firmness to her smooth white chin and a certain determined line to her, carefully etched mouth that somehow counteracted the general impression of voluptuous softness which she produced. She came toward Spike with that artificial undulating step so assiduously cultivated by ladies who are in the habit of appearing before vast audiences, hung with rhinestones, and topped by amazing creations of spiraling plumes.

"Mr. Tracy?" she inquired. The voice had originally been pure Chillecothe, but somewhere along the way it had been heavily overlaid with the accent so commonly heard on the English drawing-room stage. Spike bowed low in his most Continental manner and brushed her outstretched hand with his lips. Miss Keating smiled the smile she reserved for managers and millionaires. As a matter of fact, Miss Keating was sure that this handsome young man with the charming manner was doubtless one of the two, perhaps both, which was all the better.

"Won't you—sit down," she asked in her best manner.

"Sorry," Spike apologized, "but I really can't. As a matter of fact I'm in a frightful hurry. I just dropped in to pick you up and take you out for a drive with me, and I assure you there isn't a moment to lose."

"But really—" Miss Keating protested, but she was obviously pleased with the unaccountable behavior of this strange young man. "But really—Mr.—ah, Tracy," she refreshed her memory from his card which she still held in her hand "I don't quite understand."

"I can quite believe that my request is unusual and precipitate, but run along and get your coat on and I'll explain while we're riding."

But Miss Keating had apparently no intention of running along. Instead she sank gracefully into a chair, carefully disposing her various comely members to achieve the best possible display.

"You are a strange young man, aren't you?" and she smiled archly.

"Dearie, you don't know the half of it. But I'm not half as strange as the young men and old ones too that are going to be up here in about five or ten minutes."

"And just what do you mean?" Miss Keating stretched herself like a sinuous cat, and laid one white hand on Spike's cuff.

"I mean that the district attorney and the chief of the homicide squad are probably on their way up here right now to question you in connection with the Cecily Thane murder."

The effect of these words on Miss Audrey Keating were not unlike a shock of electricity. She sat bolt upright in her chair and her baby blue eyes grew suddenly frightened and staring. Worse still, when she spoke she had forgotten her English comedy-drama accent and had reverted to pure Chillecothe.

"Wha—what do you mean?"

"Exactly what I said. And if you're wise you'll come with me before they get here."

"But how do I know—but what—but what you—"

"Here!" Spike shoved a paper into her hand. "I neglected to present my letter of introduction."

She snatched the paper from him and read the few scribbled lines: "Audrey: I think this is a regular guy, but I'm not sure. Do what he says and he'll keep you out of trouble—maybe. Tommy Spencer."

For a moment she stood undecided, crunching the paper in her hands. Then suddenly she rushed out of the room. In not more than three minutes she was back again with her coat and a small close hat that came far down over her eyes. When her coat collar was turned up her face was almost hidden.

Not until they were in the taxicab which Spike had held in readiness at the door, and were driving slowly through the Park did she speak again. Then she turned abruptly to him.

"Who are you anyway?"

"My name is Tracy."

"The district attorney!" she gasped

"My dear young lady, why, I ask you, does the name of the district attorney strike such terror to your heart?"

"Why, what, do you mean? I'm not afraid. I've nothing to be afraid of." She spoke quickly, as if in a vain endeavor to convince herself of what she was saying.

"Then why look so scared?"

"Say, listen," she appealed "What's the idea? What do you want with me?"

"Well, first of all, perhaps I had better correct the mistaken impression you're under. I am not the district attorney."

The girl seemed visibly to melt with relief. "Then who are you?"

"I'm his brother. No, no—don't mistake me," he went on quickly as she once more grew wary. "We've really nothing much in common outside of our parents. Richard thinks life is a great legal problem and I think it's a rightfully amusing show. However, just at present we do have a mutual interest—the Thane murder case."

He paused and looked out of the corner of his eye at his companion. She was sitting very still, her hands folded in her lap, her fingers clasped in, A tight nervous grip.

"Would you mind awfully telling me what you know about it?"

She did not answer.

"Because if you don't," be went on quietly, "I'll take you back home and by that time my brother and his dear friend, Inspector Herschman, will probably be there with the cortege of newspaper reporters and photographers that have been following them around this week."

"Please—please, don't get me into this." Impulsively she grabbed his arm "I can't afford to get mixed up in the newspapers in a murder case."

"My dear girl, you simply confound all my preconceived notions about actresses. I always thought publicity was an asset."

"But not this kind. Not a murder case. Look what's happened to the actresses that have been mixed up in murder cases."

"Well then," he continued philosophically, "you'd best tell papa all. That's really your only way out."

Suddenly he turned on her that charming, beguiling smile which had melted the hearts of scores of females on both sides of the Atlantic. Gently he took one of her stiff hands in his. When he spoke again his voice carried that note described by our more impassioned novelists as low and vibrant.

"Can't you—trust me?"

The histrionics of the situation were too much for Miss Keating even in the midst of her fright.

"Can I?" Once more she was in command of her comedy-drama manner.

For reply Spike only gave her hand a long, understanding pressure as if his feelings could not be put into words. Then gently he released it and reached for his cigarette case as if to restore their relationship to a more casual basis.

Reluctantly Miss Keating accepted a cigarette and let her glance travel over her companion. Not even the realization that he was neither a millionaire, nor a manager, but was rather the brother of the district attorney could quite remove the satisfaction from her appraisal.

"What do you want to know?"

"Everything you know."

"But I don't know anything really."

"Tell me, for instance, how you happened to be acquainted with Mrs. Thane."

"Oh, I really wasn't acquainted with her. I met her on a party one night."

"Do you recall the exact circumstances?"

"No. I go to a good many parties, you know. And you know how you meet people."

"Well then, perhaps you can tell me this, did you introduce Tommy Spencer to Mrs. Thane before or after you started—ah—going about with Mr. Thane?"

The girl stopped suddenly in the middle of a long exhale of smoke and the hand which held her cigarette trembled. "What do you mean—going about with Mr. Thane?"

"It's quite useless to ask such unnecessary rhetorical questions, my girl," Spike assured her.

"I'm sure I don't know what you're talking about," she said defiantly.

"Of course you know what I'm talking about. You know as well as I do that I am referring to the fact that it's fairly common knowledge that you and Elton Thane have reached a certain stage of intimacy where—"

"That's a lie."

"What's a lie?"

"What you just said."

"But really I haven't said anything."

"You just said that Elton Thane and I—" She broke off uncertainly. Her Chillecothe training had not endowed her with words sufficiently euphemistic for such a delicate situation

"You know, my dear," Spike went on, "you'd much better come right out and tell me the truth or I shall think the worst. The very worst," he emphasized "Here I find you, a beautiful girl, who has not been working for six months and yet you are living in an apartment that doesn't cost a cent under $300 a month. There's really only one conclusion to draw."

"Is that so? Well, let me tell you something. You're all wet."

"Yes?"

"Yes, that's what I said. I'm not that kind of a girl."

"No?"

"No. A guy's not getting me until he gets me with a wedding ring around my finger. I've seen too many dames all set up in nice apartments and just settling down and enjoying themselves, and about the time they begin to get too fat to get back into a show or get another man, the guy up and leaves them—flat—cold."

"Really? How brutally heartless."

"I've seen it done too many times to get caught. Little Audrey's too smart for that."

"So I suppose you told Mr. Thane that until he could divorce his wife and marry you with full pomp and circumstance, you would allow him only the privilege of providing you with a luxurious living, for which he would get nothing in return but the charm of your companionship."

For a moment the girl said nothing. Then reluctantly she surrendered. "Yes, that's it. You're pretty smart, aren't you?"

Spike turned upon her a look of flashing admiration. "My dear, beside you, I am a low-grade moron. To get away with what you're getting away with requires no mere surface sophistication like mine. It requires genius. But tell me—did Mr. Thane accept this arrangement?"

"There wasn't anything else for him to do"

"And now I suppose that with Mrs. Thane's death, there will be nothing to prevent marriage?"

"Well, we'll wait a little while, anyway, just to make it look better."

"How did you two happen to meet?"

"Some business men I know gave a party and asked me, and three of the other girls in the show I was playing in, and he was there."

"And since then you have been—friends?"

"Yes."

"But I still don't quite understand how Tommy Spencer got dragged in."

"I dragged him in. Mr. Thane was always afraid his wife would find out about him going out with me and I said that was simple. Just keep her busy with some one else. Get her a boy friend; and I got Tommy."

Spike sighed. "It's all distressingly commercial. But weren't you afraid of meeting them when you were out with Thane?"

"No. I know pretty much what night clubs Tommy works—he gets a rake-off from the clubs, you know—and we stayed away from them. But then we didn't go to clubs much. Just dinner and a show afterward. Mr. Thane's sort of a quiet person."

"Yes, that was my impression of him. I should hardly have picked him as a person to your taste."

"What do you mean," she bridled. "Just because a girl's been on the stage every one thinks she's wild and doesn't care for a nice, refined life, with a man that's got plenty of—that—"

"A good provider," Spike supplied. "I think I understand." He smiled and Miss Keating looked hurt.

"Tell me, did Mr. Thane ever try to get a divorce?"

"No."

"And yet he professed himself eager to marry you?"

"Yes."

"Strange, isn't it?"

"Well, he always said that somehow he just never, could bring himself to it. I used to tell him he was a fool. He could have got one easy as not. We've had a lot of quarrels on that point. But then, I figured, well, if he's satisfied with present arrangements, I should worry."

"Quite sensible of you, I'm sure. But tell me, Miss Keating, what do you mean, 'he could have got one easy as not?'"

She turned on him a look of surprise. "Why, don't you know? This Fennel fellow. He and Mrs. Thane have been lovers for years."

". . . lovers for years. . . ."

"Oh, quite!" Spike remarked, but his nonchalant manner belied the sudden excited click which his brain had given, at the three words . . . *"lovers for years". . . .*

Two hours later, Spike was waiting for the district attorney and the inspector when they came back to Headquarters, both of them mumbling reproaches to each other in a disgruntled manner.

"We went after this Audrey woman," the district attorney explained to Spike. "Her last name's Keating. But she wasn't home. Herschman's having the place watched."

"I hardly think that will do much good," Spike remarked. "I have a feeling that Miss Keating is not going to return for some time. She tells me that she hates newspaper photographers and policemen."

Herschman whirled on his heel and faced Spike. "What do you mean?"

"I mean I've just been out driving with Miss Keating and she asked me to drop her at the corner of Fifty-ninth and Eighth Avenue, and the last I saw of her she was disappearing into the downtown subway. I pointed out to her that her apartment would undoubtedly be favored by a visit from the police and she seemed appalled at the prospect."

"You mean you had hold of her and you let her go?"

"Just her hand."

"No funny business. Where is she now?"

"I have no idea."

"Say, lissen, brother," Herschman began savagely, "what are you trying to do, double-cross us. I'm getting damn tired of your meddling. What business have you got, I'd like to know, butting in and balling things—"

"Inspector," Spike broke in, "remember your blood pressure."

"Damn my blood pressure!"

"You know, old thing, I had an idea that Miss Keating was just what she turned out to be—a devastating combination of ignorance and shrewdness—something that not even the combined legal and police minds of New York could batter through. Sex appeal was what was needed, and if I do say so myself, I rather feel that in that respect I have a slight edge on you and Richard."

"Damn your sex appeal! How did you find out where she lived? It wasn't in the telephone book and it took us two hours to track her down."

"Oh, I got her address from a friend of mine. Really, you know, our little drive was most revealing. Acting again like the low cad that I am, I gained her confidence and then pried loose some very interesting information."

While Herschman sat in glowering silence, Spike began the story of his afternoon's adventures. But when he came to the revelation of the unique financial relations between Thane and Miss Keating, the inspector suddenly grew alert

"You see," Spike explained, "she's a very, very clever girl."

"Yeah, and I also see that Elton Thane's a very, very guilty man." He rose in sudden decision.

"Where are you going?" the district attorney inquired.

"I'm going up to arrest Elton Thane for the murder of his wife. There you are. Motive absolutely proved and clear. He wanted to marry this Keating girl and collect on the money he'd been spending on her, and he couldn't as long as his wife was holding that check on him. And he couldn't get the check from her, so—" He made a gesture with his hands to indicate that it was all as plain as day.

"But you forget," the district attorney reminded him, "that Thane couldn't possibly have done it. He was at Dr. Partridge's from ten minutes to twelve on. And Spencer was with Mrs. Thane until twelve."

Herschman stopped abruptly in the act of reaching for his hat. As he considered the district attorney's words the determined set to his jaw gave way.

"Yes, that's right," he admitted. Then he turned to Spike with a disgruntled snap. "Well, go on with your story. Is that all?"

"Not quite," and Spike continued. As he drew to the end of his account he asked for the blotter which, had been removed from Cecily Thane's writing table the morning after she was murdered. Holding it up to a small looking-glass the letters were plain.

Taking a pencil he sketched in lightly the missing letters and handed it over to Tracy and Herschman. Now the reflection read:

"And that my dears, is what Mrs. Thane said in the kind letter of sympathy she wrote to Mrs. Fennel last Monday afternoon. Under the circumstances I think we ought to have another go at the Fennels—Mortimer Fennel in particular."

XV. NINA FENNEL FAILS TO EXPLAIN

ONCE more the three men stood outside the Fennel apartment and waited for an answer to their ring—the district attorney, Spike and the inspector. They had to ring twice before the slatternly maid at last opened the door to them and led them almost as a matter of course into the front room.

A few minutes later Nina Fennel appeared in the doorway. There were deep circles of weariness under her eyes and her heavy dark hair, sliding low on her neck, seemed to elongate the lines of her face.

"Well?" she said as she stood in the doorway.

"Miss Fennel, we've come to see you—and your father." The district attorney put particular emphasis on the last three words.

"I'm afraid it's just about as useless this time as the last," she said in a tired voice. "My mother's condition is unchanged."

"I'm very sorry to hear that, I'm sure, but I must insist that we see your father too, this time."

"No. It is impossible." She stood in the doorway, blocking the way. Herschman rose and came toward her.

"No, it's not impossible," he said. "Not if I have to go down to your mother's room and bring him out myself."

"No—no!" A terrified look leaped into her blazing eyes. But the inspector never wavered. He took her arm in a grip that seemed to the observer a gentle one, but it was like steel. His eyes bored into her. She faltered. Then suddenly the backbone went out of her.

"All right," she said, "I'll call him." And she turned in defeat and walked down the dark hall.

Mortimer Fennel, if he had looked weak and tired that first morning on which he had faced the district attorney, now seemed as if he had scarcely the strength to bring one dragging foot after the other.

"You—you wanted to see me again?"

"Yes, you—and your daughter," Tracy said.

"You realize—that my wife—"

"I understand, and I regret greatly that we have to intrude at this particular time; but there are some things that we must ask you to repeat, Mr. Fennel. Please tell us again, every movement you made on the night Cecily Thane was murdered."

And again Fennel related his story of the previous Monday night. It was the same as he had told them once before.

"And you are quite sure, are you, that your little call on the Thanes had nothing at all to do with a letter that Mrs. Thane wrote Monday afternoon to your wife?"

"Why—yes, I told you that before." His voice was hoarse.

"And you're quite sure that after leaving the Thane house at nine-thirty you did not return to it later on."

"Quite sure"

"And you came directly home"

"No," put in the girl quickly. "He walked around a while."

"I'm not asking you," Herschman snapped. "I'm asking your father. You came directly home?"

"No—I walked around a while."

"How long?"

"Oh, I don't know."

"Half an hour?"

"No. Longer than that."

"What time did you get back here?"

"It was—it must have been quite late. The elevator wasn't running."

"And you, Miss Fennel, you're also quite sure, I suppose, that you left there not later than ten o'clock?"

Fennel shot a sudden surprised glance at his daughter.

"But—but she wasn't there," he protested.

"Yes, Father," the girl said, "I told them I was."

"What was your idea, Mr. Fennel, in lying to us, telling us that you were alone in the Thane house?"

"I—I didn't want to get Nina mixed up in it."

"What do you mean, in it?"

"Oh, all the publicity and scandal and—" Mortimer Fennel made a hopeless, weary gesture.

Herschman turned back to the girl. "You're sure, are you, that you left there not later than ten o'clock?"

Her chin went up suddenly in a defiant gesture. "I am quite sure."

Again the corners of the inspector's mouth turned up slightly and the cat-and-mouse expression, indicative of extreme pleasure spread over his face. He paused. Then slowly he spoke, boring the words in as he faced Nina Fennel.

"Since you're so ready with your answers, Miss Fennel, maybe you can explain why you went to Mr. Tommy Spencer's apartment last Monday night shortly after one, about the hour you told us you were 'just walking' along Riverside Drive."

Nina Fennel said nothing. The gesture of defiance seemed suddenly to freeze on her face, and Herschman went, on relentlessly. "And maybe you can also tell why on Tuesday afternoon you threw a revolver into a northbound sand car along the New York Central tracks."

Slowly she lifted a trembling hand to her mouth and her eyes grew wide with terror.

Herschman's voice grew louder. "And you don't need to tell me what Mrs. Thane wrote to your mother last Monday afternoon, because I know. She told your mother that she and your father 'had been lovers for—'"

Suddenly there was a stifled shriek. Nina Fennel flung herself on the detective and clapped both her trembling hands over his mouth.

"For God's sake—no—don't—" and her terror-stricken eyes signaled down the dark hall. There was a deathly silence. Not a soul spoke. All eyes were on the girl. And then like an eerie, weird wail came the voice, weak, palsied with sickness.

"M—Mortimer!"

The girl and her father looked at each other, their eyes exchanging desperate messages.

"Father—go—" and she pointed down the dark hall. Mortimer Fennel stumbled out of the room toward the faint, piteous wail.

When he had gone, the girl shut the door behind him and stumbled to a chair and sank weakly into it, as if her legs would no longer support her. She leaned her head on her hand and did not face them as she spoke.

"Well—go on."

"But it's your turn to go on," the inspector reminded her. "You haven't yet answered my questions. Why did you go to Tommy Spencer's apartment last Monday night and write him a note in which you said, 'Something terrible has happened.'"

"I—I thought—I mean I thought he could help me—about the letter that Mrs. Thane wrote to my mother."

"And how could he help you?"

"I—I—didn't know. He knew Mrs. Thane so well and I thought—why, I thought he might be able to do something to stop her."

"But that doesn't explain why you went to such pains to dispose of a revolver the following afternoon. Why did you do that?"

"I—I thought—" She broke off suddenly and pressed her trembling lips together.

"You thought what?"

"I—I don't know."

"You don't know why you threw the revolver away. Whose revolver was it?"

"It—it's just one that's been around the house for a long time."

"It wasn't by any chance a .38 caliber Colt?"

"I don't know. I—I didn't notice."

"But why did you throw it away?"

"Oh—I never did like guns—and I just thought—I'd—I'd get rid of it."

The inspector paused to consider the situation for a moment. Then quickly he made up his mind. "Your explanations, Miss Fennel, are not satisfactory. I'm holding you as a material witness in this case—without bail. You and your—"

"No—no, please. Let me go. I'll go. Don't take him away from her. She's dying. She may not live till morning She's—Oh, God—"

Suddenly she collapsed forward on to the arm if her chair, a piteous figure, weeping hysterically, pleading.

"Don't you think, Inspector," the district attorney broke in in a quiet voice, "that it will be sufficient to hold the girl?"

XVI. A Confession

"WOULD it be impertinent to inquire," said Spike as he slouched lazily in an easy-chair in his brother's office the following morning, "now that you've got the three of them in jail what are you going to do with them?"

"What are we going to do with them?" the inspector repeated brusquely. "Why, we're going to—ah—"

"Yes, I thought as much."

"Lissen, young fellow," he burst out.

"Call me Spike, old man, just Spike. Neat and to the point."

But Herschman apparently did not get the point, for he relapsed into moody silence.

"I sympathize with you," Spike admitted with feeling. "I really do. Spencer talks too much. Miss Fennel won't talk at all—beyond a certain point. And Griffis is too scared to be of much account. That being the case, I'll take a hand myself."

He settled himself more comfortably and lit a cigarette. "Where do we stand? Well, it seems pretty certain that on the night Cecily Thane was murdered, her house was simply teeming with people who had no particular fancy for her. Who, in fact, wouldn't be at all distressed with her out of the picture.

"No. 1—her husband who, while waiting to be legally free, is put to the impertinent expense of supporting his girl friend without getting anything out of it. When he asked his wife for a divorce, she probably reminded him of the forged check which she held and told him to try and get it.

"No. 2—Mortimer Fennel and his Amazonian daughter, Nina, naturally have a grudge against the murdered lady, seeing as how she tried to spill the beans to their ailing wife and mother that for the past fifteen years Mortimer has not been all that a devoted husband should be. They probably intercepted that letter before it ever got to Mrs. Fennel, but they were afraid that another time, Mrs. Thane might be more successful.

"No 3—George Griffis who is hard up and needs money and has an ancient but quite understandable grudge against Cecily for helping her husband nick him out of $50,000."

"You forget," the district attorney, put in, "that Thane repaid him that money."

"So Thane says. But George seems to have suffered a lapse of memory on this particular point. George didn't seem at all upset his by sister's death. And that is that."

"You forget Tommy Spencer," the inspector reminded him.

"No, I didn't forget Tommy. I can't quite decide about him. The fact remains that despite the disparity in their social position and disposition, Miss Nina Fennel went out of her way to meet him and has since encouraged him. And despite Tommy's obvious charms, they are not the sort I think would appeal to a girl of Miss Fennel's type. To be very frank, I'm rather of the opinion—"

But Spike got no further. It was at this particular junction that they were interrupted by the district attorney's secretary. "A gentleman to see you," he announced. "Mr. Fennel."

"There's going to be no bail for that girl," Herschman declared. "If the old guy thinks that he's going to come around and get the girl out, he's all wet."

Tracy nodded to Lovelace to bring Fennel in.

As Mortimer Fennel stood in the doorway facing the district attorney, the inspector and the insouciant young man, even the most casual observer would have been struck by the change in him. His nervousness was gone, his trembling hands were still. His whole being seemed diffused with a great despair, but a despair which he no longer fought. It was as if he had been clinging desperately to something, but had at last surrendered, quietly as one who realizes the futility of struggle. His shoulders sagged with defeat.

The district attorney indicated a chair, and Fennel dragged his faltering feet across the floor and sank into it. For a moment no one said anything. Then Tracy spoke. "Well, Mr. Fennel?"

Fennel raised his haggard, despairing eyes "I have come to get my daughter," he said simply, and his voice was like something from the dead

"That is impossible," Herschman broke in. "She's held without bail."

"Yes, I know. But you must let her go."

"Let her go?"

"Her mother is dying I have just come from her bedside. The doctor says that she can't last until noon."

"Look here, Fennel, you don't need to come pulling that—"

But Fennel held up his hand and cut him short. "My, daughter did not murder Mrs. Thane. She knows nothing about it." He spoke the words in a calm, even voice, but he closed his eyes as he said them. Then even more quietly, even more calmly, he went on,   "I did it."

For a moment there was a dead silence in the room. Spike, Tracy, and Herschman had suddenly leaned forward in their chairs, staring at the man in front of them, scarcely breathing.

"Yes, I did it." He opened his eyes and looked about him. "If you will bring a stenographer in here, I would like to dictate my confession. That is—I think that is the usual way, isn't it?" There was something tragic and piteous in the utterly calm manner with which he sought to comply with precedent.

Without a word Herschman rose and walked quietly to the door, summoning Lovelace from the outer office.

When the secretary had seated himself at a small table, Fennel looked inquiringly once more at the district attorney.

"It is customary, is it not, to give a brief description of yourself in—in such cases?"

The district attorney nodded.

In the same colorless voice, Fennel proceeded; slowly so that Lovelace might have no difficulty in getting each word.

"I am Mortimer Fennel, forty-six years old, commercial artist, free lance. Twenty-four years ago I married Maybelle Comminger, and a year later our daughter, Nina, was born. My wife has been an invalid since then."

It was as if he were merely reciting something he had learned by heart, as if he had written it down beforehand and memorized it. With never a pause for a word, never a single fumbling for a phrase he went on.

"When my daughter was eight years old I met Cecily Thane and her husband. She was dissatisfied with life and so was I. We became—lovers. Seven years ago her husband discovered our relationship, but it made no difference to him.

"During the last three years, my feelings changed, so that I no longer cared to continue the relationship, but Mrs. Thane insisted that if I did not do so, she would tell my wife. In spite of my conduct during the last fifteen years, I have always felt for my wife a greater love than I have ever had for any woman, and she has never for a moment suspected my infidelity. My daughter, Nina, however, has known the truth for several years, and has aided me in keeping it from her mother.

"The relationship between me and Cecily Thane at length became so strained that in desperation I told her that I would never see her again. Last Monday afternoon she sent my wife a letter by special messenger, telling her the whole sordid story. Fortunately my daughter intercepted it.

"Together we went to Mrs. Thane's house Monday night, to plead with her to desist. I did not wish my daughter to be drawn into it unless I could help it. When

I found that Mrs. Thane was not there I summoned my daughter to the house. I don't know why I did this except perhaps that I have always been a weak character, and I have always leaned heavily on her youth and strength.

"I was in such a wrought-up state that my daughter forced me to leave the house and said she would remain and deal with Mrs. Thane. A half hour later, feeling that it was useless for her to wait any longer that night, she left."

Fennel paused, closed his eyes as if to summon strength for what was to follow. Then he went on, still calm, dead:

"I returned to the house at eleven o'clock and let myself in with the latchkey which I still kept from the years when I was on more friendly terms with Mrs. Thane. I hid myself in her dressing room until after she had come in with Tommy Spencer and Spencer had left.

"And after he left, I—I shot her. I took the jewels from her jewel safe to make it appear like robbery. I left the house immediately and threw the jewels wrapped in a newspaper in a garbage can. Then I came back to my home at 204 West Eighty-sixth Street.

"That—that is all."

Fennel sat now, staring straight ahead of him. Slowly he reached forth a hand and took a pen from the desk and dipped it in the inkwell. In a firm untrembling hand he wrote his name at the bottom of the long sheet which the secretary pulled from his typewriter.

And now," he said as he handed the paper to the district attorney, "will you release my daughter—immediately? She must see her mother—before—she—dies."

And very quietly Mortimer Fennel sank to the floor unconscious.

XVII. Spike Reads the *"Times"*

ON Sunday morning, the day following the confession of Mortimer Fennel, Spike stood outside Police Headquarters and hesitated. The gaudy magazine covers of a corner newsstand caught his eye, and he stopped for a paper. Strangely enough, though, it was not the screaming pink of his favorite evening tab that he selected from the array spread out on the counter, but the dignified pages of the *Times*.

Slowly he strolled down Centre Street until he came to Sherman Park. He dropped down on to one of the benches and unfolded his paper. Even the erudite *Times* had given the Thane murder confession a two-column head on the front page, for not even erudition and dignity could disregard the pitiful, moving story of Mortimer Fennel.

There it all was, the secret that both he and his daughter had so painfully guarded, spread out for the world to read and relish. And yet even amid the welter of tragedy there was one comforting thought. They had succeeded. Mrs. Mortimer Fennel had died the previous day in the arms of her daughter, even to the end unconscious of the black shadow that for fifteen years had hovered over her home.

Spike read the news columns slowly, his own knowledge of the persons involved piecing out the story that had been unearthed by the reporters. He read to the end and then put down the paper, and let his mind reconstruct the whole pitiful, tragic tale.

Mortimer Fennel, a young man in art school with dreams of the Paris salons driving his brushes, had found that a passionate but too early marriage made his plans for study abroad impossible But he had surrendered gracefully to necessity, for he had been very much in love with his young wife. Commercial art paid the rent and the grocery bills. And presently came joy and tragedy. Nina was born, and from that day on Maybelle Fennel remained an invalid, chained to a wheel chair—a sweet, gentle shadow whose physical weakness was matched only by the moral instability of her husband.

Endowed with all the intensity of an artistic temperament, his ambitions thwarted by lack of money, Mortimer Fennel soon found that he was not of the fiber of which martyrs are made. He still loved his wife with a strange, mystical tenderness. He adored his baby daughter. But the inherent weakness of his nature coupled with the desires of the flesh proved too much for him.

His acquaintance with Cecily Thane had started quite casually enough; The Thanes moved into the same apartment house in which the Fennels lived, and the common cause of tenants—lack of hot water, a broken elevator or a delinquent janitor—brought them into each other's lives

And Cecily Thane was ripe for change. Elton Thane, a salaried jewelry salesman, could not provide her with the luxuries to which her upbringing had never accustomed her, but which she desired avidly. And because her mind and her time and her life were empty, she welcomed the entrance of Mortimer Fennel. He was young, and quixotic, and good looking, and had that peculiar charm for women which weak men so frequently possess; and the hopeless state of his own family life, which offered no outlet for his passionate nature, soon resulted in a liaison.

He would have been content to let it be just that, but Cecily Thane for once in her life found herself touched by a real emotion. She wanted Mortimer Fennel and wanted him desperately—wanted him in all his poverty and weakness She had arrived at that love-is-all-and-the-world-well-lost emotional state where she would willingly have run off with him to any romantic, quixotic end of the earth which he selected.

But Mortimer Fennel was not even a strong enough character to do the cowardly thing. He longed desperately to rid his life of the trying complications of an invalid wife and an infant daughter, but he lacked even the courage to make the break. And so for fifteen years he and Cecily Thane were unmolested in their love making. By the time Elton Thane had discovered the true state of affairs, he was too engrossed in making money, in building up his own business to care—much.

At first it had piqued his pride. But gradually he found that it was after all a rather convenient arrangement. It left him more or less free to pursue his own desires. And since the time had long since passed when Cecily was any part of those desires, he let in drift. And so they drifted—drifted. And all the time Nina Fennel was growing up. At fifteen she had an instinctive dislike of the beautiful Mrs. Thane of whom her father occasionally spoke. At twenty she actively hated her, and at twenty-one she had divined the whole hateful story.

Just when she had come to know, she could not have told, no more than Mortimer Fennel could have told when he became conscious of the fact that he had gradually begun to lean on the daughter that had so recently been just a little girl, and was now a grown woman. The years of his entanglement with Cecily Thane had not dealt happily with Mortimer Fennel. It was only the strong pull of the flesh that kept him at her side, for his instinctive fastidious discernment, so ill-combined in his weak nature, showed him plainly the vacuity, of this woman. After the first year he ceased to love her, but he did not cease to desire her.

However, even desire at last becomes faint, and in Mortimer Fennel this diminishing process was premature. The swift passion of his nature had spent him, until at forty-five he found that he no longer even desired her. Upon her, the years had just the opposite effect. At thirty-eight her physical charms and her lover were slowly slipping from her. With a desperate fury she fought to recreate the old ardor; but Mortimer Fennel was weary. He wanted only the peace of his own home, and the gentle companionship of his shadowy, fading wife. He was like a runner who has run too swiftly and suddenly finds himself broken and winded with a wish for nothing but infinite rest.

She even tried the obvious device of what was apparently a new and younger lover, but in reality was only a hired dancing partner. And then with a swift rush the whole lingering tragedy of the last fifteen years had resolved itself into an imminent terror. Cecily Thane had told him that unless he returned to her she would tell his wife of the relationship which had existed between them. She had used the last and lowest weapon of a desperate woman, a woman beyond love or hate, carried away by an avenging despair—moral blackmail. She had made good her threat, but Fennel and his daughter had intercepted the letter before it reached Maybelle Fennel.

"In less than twenty-four hours after she wrote the letter to Mrs. Mortimer Fennel, Cecily Thane was found dead with a bullet through her heart."

It was a damning juxtaposition of two facts, and Spike frowned as his eyes rested on them at the end of a column. Presently he rose from the bench and slowly retraced his steps in the direction of Police Headquarters. But he did not go in. For a moment he stood uncertain, two thoughtful lines between his eyes. Then he hailed a taxi.

"Bellevue Hospital." A few moments later when the cab cut in toward the curb in front of the hospital he told the driver to wait while he went inside. In less then twenty minutes he was back. He was still puzzled and thoughtful, still hesitant as to his next move, but a certain excited eagerness had replaced his sober dejection.

"15 West Ninety-third," he directed, but a few moments later as they were driving up Second Avenue he leaned forward and gave another address. "8 West Eighty-second Street."

But when he arrived at the Thane house he did not get out. Instead, he merely sat and looked at its innocuous façade. It was as if he sought to find in some turn of masonry or woodwork, the answer to the puzzle that had brought two deep furrows between his eyes. Slowly his gaze traveled over the front of the house up and down the street . . . across . . . and at last in defeat they came to rest on the yawning maw of upturned asphalt, disjoined sewer pipe, and heavy beamed timbering that marked the site of the future subway station. The fierce, bewhiskered Irishman and the three little sweating Italians were still at work. Or at least the Italians were. The Irishman sat in magnificent detachment on an upturned keg and gave orders and stroked his Victorian whiskers.

At last with a shrug of defeat, Spike motioned the driver to go on, and the car backed out of Eighty-second Street and presently drew up in front of 15 West Ninety-third Street. As he shot up in the elevator he reflected on the last time that he had been there and the ill-fated fruit which his investigation had borne. He was met at the door of Tommy's apartment by Tommy himself. Despite the fact that he was clad only in rumpled pajamas, there was a haggard, drawn look to his face as if little sleep had come to him his first night out of jail.

"Where's your man," Spike inquired as he settled himself in a chair, and Tommy stretched out wearily on the davenport.

"I fired him. He wanted his wages and I didn't have a cent, so I gave him about $400 worth of clothes and junk and put him out. The nerve of him, and me out of jail only two hours."

"Absolutely no consideration for the feelings of a gentleman. You did quite right to fire him. But tell me, old thing, how are you feeling this morning after your week's rest cure?"

"Rotten!"

"That's extraordinary. You really should be in the pink. No late hours, and only the simple coarse fare which doctors are so frightfully keen on."

"That's not what I mean. I mean I'm feeling rotten."

"Exactly. You mean that being slightly struck with Nina Fennel, you're all cut up about her father."

Tommy nodded. "God!" he broke out suddenly. "I'd almost have rather they'd plastered it on me, than have it happen like it has."

"A very worthy and chivalrous sentiment, I'm sure. Far more than Nina Fennel deserves."

"What do you mean? 'Far, more than Nina Fennel deserves?'" Tommy bridled.

"I mean, my lad, that Nina Fennel just played up to you because she thought you might be able to help her crab Mrs. Thane's deal."

Tommy flushed hotly. "That's not true. She wouldn't do a thing like that."

"Yes, I think she would. My impression of Nina is that she's a very strong-minded and calculating girl. She simply thought you might be used as a handy tool. Just how, I don't imagine she had all worked out."

"Yes," Tommy admitted disconsolately. "I guess you're right. She's not my class. But anyway I'm sorry for her sake that her father killed Mrs. Thane."

"The sentiment does credit to your kindness of heart but not to your perspicacity."

"That's all right with me. Whatever it is you're talking about."

"I mean, my dear fellow, that Mortimer Fennel did not kill Mrs. Thane."

"What?"

"Really, Tommy, you are difficult. You seem to understand neither my best four-dollar words nor the simple forty-cent variety. I said, Mortimer Fennel did not kill Mrs. Thane."

"But he confessed."

"Of course. He partakes of your chivalrous nature."

"But if he didn't do it, what's the idea?"

Spike settled himself more comfortably and lit a cigarette before he spoke again. "It's too bad, Tommy, that you don't understand human psychology better. Then you'd realize that for the first time in his life, Mortimer Fennel is really being noble. And the usual thing has happened. He has overdone it.

"All his life he has been a weak soul, continually leaning on some one else. Before she fell ill, he probably leaned on his wife. And then he leaned on Cecily Thane. And when he grew too old and tired for the rather arduous attention which she demanded, he leaned on his daughter. Leaned heavily. That, perhaps, is why Nina is such a strong-minded person. She has had to be."

"Well, I don't see anything noble in all that."

"Of course not. That's just the point. Mortimer Fennel is suffering from an attack of accumulated decency. All his life he has been a weakling. And like many weaklings, he has experienced a delayed realization of just what an egg he has been. So he's making a noble gesture of expiation. He's doing it because he has at last realized that he's no good, and that the best thing he can do is to give up his worthless life to save his daughter."

"What do you mean, 'save his daughter'?" Tommy was suddenly alert, defiant.

"I mean save her from the electric chair."

"You don't mean to tell me that you think Nina did it?"

"Her father thinks so and I imagine he is rather better acquainted with her than we are."

"Do you think so?"

"My dear fellow, I never jump to conclusions— especially when there are so many alternatives. Just because I am convinced that Mortimer Fennel did not do it, is no sign that I think his daughter did. Especially in view of the fact that there were a number of other people in the house during the evening."

A sudden, wary silence seemed to descend upon Tommy. He tamped out his cigarette and sat immobile, only his eyes moving, shifting about the room.

"Well," he said finally in a dogged, voice. "Go ahead. Give me the works. I'm used to it by this time."

Spike laughed. "You sound as though you were a criminal and I was a member of the third degree squad of the police department."

"Well, you think I am, don't you?"

"I admit the possibility. But I admit other possibilities, too. After all there were other people in the house that night beside you."

Spike drew from his pocket a small memorandum book and a fountain pen. "Suppose we're very businesslike, and put things down neatly in black and white.

"There was first of all, the maid."

"No. 1—the maid," he wrote.

"And then there was the husband—the outraged husband. For years his wife has been unfaithful to him. But because he was a nice meal ticket she wouldn't divorce him. And in the meantime he had fallen for some one else. Excellent reason for murder.

"And then there is the boy friend—the hired boy friend. His record shows that he's traveling under an assumed name, and that once before he was involved in a similar case but was released for lack of evidence."

"But I'm telling you that I never had a thing to do with that Schlockenhass case. Not anything more than I had to do with this one."

"Tommy, my dear, do try to look at it more objectively. I'm merely putting things down as any right-minded, reasonably suspicious person would regard them.

"And then there is brother, who finds himself in serious financial difficulties. Unless he has five thousand dollars he'll go bust. And his sister refuses to give it to him.

"No. 4 is Nina Fennel. She—"

"But she didn't do it!" Tommy broke in vehemently.

"I'm telling you, I—"

"Tommy, spare me, spare me," and Spike held up his hand in a pained gesture. "Don't, I beg of you, tell me that you did it. Things are altogether too complicated already with one gentleman confessing to the dastardly deed to save the beautiful Nina, without another one messing things up."

"Oh, well!" Tommy gave a helpless shrug to his shoulders and settled once more, into gloom.

"So you see, old thing," Spike went on, "there were at least five persons in the house that night that might reasonably have been interested in Cecily Thane's death. Take yourself, for instance."

"All right, take me if you insist on being stubborn. I've told you everything. I've come absolutely clean."

"I know, but there are still a few little puzzles in my mind. I wish you'd repeat, if you don't mind, just exactly what you did after the maid brought in the cocktail shaker and the ice."

"Well, I mixed up some drinks and we had a round apiece. I had this date I was telling you about and I had to hurry off and so I left."

"Just where was Mrs. Thane when you left the room?"

"She was lying back in the chaise longue."

"And you went directly downstairs and rang for the maid to bring your hat and coat and stick?"

"Yes. And then I went out the door and started down toward Central Park West to get a cab. And at the corner of Central Park West and Eighty-second Street I hailed— No, wait a minute. I came out of the house." Tommy went back over his story meticulously, trying earnestly not to omit any detail however slight. "I came out of the house and I stopped a few minutes looking at that subway excavation.

"They were working with a drill you know, one of those things that bores down into rock and makes such a God-awful noise A big fellow with whiskers, and two or three other fellows. And I stopped watching them for a few minutes and pretty soon they quit work and then I went on up to Central Park West and got a cab."

"Have you any idea how long you stood watching the subway workmen?"

"Oh, five—ten minutes. You know, how it is when you're looking into excavations."

"And while you were standing there did you notice any one going into the Thane house?"

"No. I wasn't looking at the house, I was watching the hunkies."

"Very well. Go on."

"Well, I got the cab and drove down to the Club Paradis and met my friends there. I don't remember just what time it was, but I had three or four drinks, and got a little tight, and danced a while, and then I went home and went to bed. And that's the honest-to-God's truth."

For a moment Spike said nothing but sat in silence digesting these facts. "Then why," he said presently in a quiet tone, "why immediately on reading of the murder of Cecily Thane in the *Graphic* the next morning did you dress hastily and go out and dispose of your gun?"

Tommy's hand in the act of lifting his cigarette to his ups paused in mid-air. Then slowly he lowered it.

"What do you mean" he said.

"Really," Spike protested. "It's difficult to speak any plainer. You'd best answer me right off. Why did you go out and dispose of your gun and where did you dispose of it?"

"Oh, all right—all right," Tommy at last gave in with a surly air. "A fellow that's been in a jam like I'd been in with the Schiockenhass woman doesn't like to get caught in another one. And the less guns you have around you at a time like that the healthier it is for you."

"Oh, quite."

"Especially when the one you've got happens to be the same caliber as the one that did the murder."

"I can quite understand your apprehension."

"So I wrapped it up in a piece of newspaper and tied it with a string and threw it in a garbage can."

"But surely you know that a pistol expert could tell whether the shot had been fired from your gun or from another."

"Oh, do you think so?" Tommy laughed derisively. "Sure, the one I'd hire for the defense would get up and swear that it wasn't, and the expert hired by the cops would get up and swear that it was; and who's going to tell which one is lying. No, no, dearie, I know my stuff. By this time I hope the damn thing's at the bottom of Jamaica Bay."

"Undoubtedly is," Spike said and rose to go. "Well, old dear, you've been willing, if not very helpful." But at the door, after he had gathered up his hat and stick and gloves, he paused. "By the way, your undue haste the morning you read of the murder of Mrs. Thane was not in any degree heightened by reading the note which Nina Fennel left for you the night before, was it?"

Tommy's hand paused halfway to his mouth. His eyes met Spike's and slowly, they were invaded by dread and apprehension, which he strove valiantly to conceal.

"Wha—what do you mean?" he said at length striving to be casual.

"Never mind," Spike said airily. "It really doesn't matter," and he walked out closing the door softly behind him on Tommy Spencer's face which had suddenly gone a pale, ghastly green.

XVIII. Spike Takes an Eye-Opener

OUTSIDE the apartment building Spike paused once again in indecision. The heavy frown between his eyes was even deeper now. At length he summoned a taxi and gave the address of the Thane house. But neither his gestures nor his commands were at all sure. He was still groping. Still playing for an off chance.

At the corner of Eighty-second Street and Columbus Avenue he dismissed the taxi and walked the half block to the Thane house, hesitated once more with his foot upon the lower step, and then turned irresolutely toward the subway excavation. For a few moments he leaned against the board railing which kept chance pedestrians from falling into the hole, and watched the workmen.

For once the bewhiskered Irishman seemed to be taking part in the proceedings. A large and stubborn bowlder clung tenaciously to its rocky moorings, and the men were laboriously prying it loose with a crowbar. All four of them heaved and sweated at the iron rod, and at last with a great cracking sound the under strata gave way and the bowlder shivered loose.

The Irishman straightened up and wiped a dripping brow with a very red but none too clean handkerchief. Having done his share of the manual labor, he retreated once more to his upturned keg and proceeded to supply the mental direction of the enterprise. The steady persistence with which Spike gazed in his direction at last had its telepathic effect. He rose from his keg and picked his way over the rocky floor of the excavation until he was directly in front of the observer.

"Hot work," he said just by way of opening the conversation, and indicated the bowlder.

Spike nodded in sympathy and inquired politely when the new project would be in operation.

"Not for two or three years. Maybe four."

"Frightfully slow, don't you think?"

"Slow? Say, brother, we been working three shifts every twenty-four hours for the last six months. We're burning it up."

"You're always on the day shift?"

"We take turns. Up to a week ago I was on the 4 to 12 shift, but I changed two days ago to the 9 to 4."

Spike's eye lighted up with a sudden gleam of interest. "Then you must have been working here the night—" He nodded significantly in the direction of the Thane house.

"Yes, right here all the time, thinking how nothing exciting ever happens, and not twenty feet away from me a murder." The workman laughed heartily at the quaint humor of life. "Funny," he went on, relishing the idea of discussing the astonishing events of which he might be said to be a part. "Funny, but I always thought that that Spencer fellow did it, 'til I read in the papers this morning that Fennel fellow's confession."

"Really?" Spike opened his cigarette case and shared it with the man. "What made you think that? You know I'm frightfully interested in murders."

"Well," the workman went on puffing contentedly between words. "You know the night that Fennel did the job? Well, along about twelve, little before, I noticed some one hanging over the railing, just like you are now. But there's so many people that come along and gawp at us that I didn't pay much attention. And I wouldn't have noticed this fellow only one of the hunkies here lets fly his pick by mistake, and the head comes off and shoots up, in the direction of this fellow that's leaning over the rail.

"And then I looked up and got a good look at him right in the face. The pick head came just about two inches of hitting him. Of course at the time I didn't think much of it, but the next day when I see it in the paper, and see his picture I remembered.

"And then I thought, godamighty what a nervy bastard! Shooting a lady and then coming out and standing around ten minutes looking at a hunch of hunkies excavating. If I'd just committed a murder, I'd be running as fast as I could in the opposite direction."

"That does seem the natural thing to do," Spike admitted; but his reply was perfunctory as if he were thinking with one corner of his mind and paying little attention to what he was saying aloud. Then he looked sharply at the workman and posed a question.

"You say the night shift ends at twelve?" The workman nodded.

"Promptly? You don't ever linger on for a few minutes?"

The workman laughed. "Say, brother, when you been working eight hours you don't do not even one minute of overtime if you don't have to. You quit prompt the second that little bell rings." And he motioned in the direction of the timbering on the opposite side of the excavation where the small metal circle of an electric bell gleamed. "It goes off automatic all up and down the line, here. Got it hitched up to Western Union."

"Really? How extremely efficient. And so, on the night Mrs. Thane was murdered you went off duty promptly at twelve—after young Tommy Spencer had been standing here watching you for about ten minutes?"

"Yes, we—Say, young fellow," the workman broke off uneasily. "Are you a cop?"

"My dear fellow, I hardly know whether to be insulted in appearance or mentality."

"Eh?"

"I say, it's quite all right." And with a thoughtful pursing of his lips Spike suddenly stepped away from the excavation and bounded up the steps of the Thane house and rang the bell.

"Say, what the hell?" The workman stood open-mouthed, puzzled, as he watched the door close on Spike's back.

Inside Spike found a new and strange servant—a butler, who discreetly took his name, and his hat, and his stick, and informed him when he asked for Mr. Thane that Mr. Thane was at his uptown shop and would not be back until the evening Spike hesitated for a moment and was about to retrieve his hat and stick, when he thought better of it.

"Then may I speak to Emma for a moment?"

The butler nodded but it was plain that he did not approve of the master's visitors consorting with servant girls.

Spike went into the drawing-room and in a few moments Emma appeared. When she saw him her face lighted up with a smile that was slightly coquettish. It was as if the confession of Mortimer Fennel had in some mysterious fashion restored to Emma her old grip on life.

No longer was she wary, frightened.

"Oh, Mr. Tracy," she said, but the sudden business-like greeting of Spike soon made it plain that his errand had not the personal connotations which she had hoped.

"Tell me, Emma," he said; on the night that Mrs. Thane was murdered, did you—" He broke off and appeared to reconsider. When at length he spoke again it was with the disarming airiness which usually characterized his conversation.

"Tell me, Emma, are you acquainted with Miss Nina Fennel?"

"No, sir."

"Had she as far as you know ever been to see Mrs. Thane?"

"No, sir."

"Quite sure about that?"

"Yes, sir. If she ever was here, I never let her in."

"But do you always answer the door?"

"No, sir. Just when we haven't any butler."

"And you have a new butler now. Very charming chap, isn't he?"

Emma blushed slightly and merely nodded. It was plain that she too had felt the new butler's charm.

"When did the old butler leave?"

"Just a few days before Mrs. Thane was mur—About a week ago Thursday."

"Of his own accord?"

"No, sir. He and Mr. Thane had a quarrel and he got fired."

"You don't by any chance know what the quarrel was about"

"No, sir. Hickson, that was the old butler, didn't say. He just said he got a dirty deal."

"And it was Hickson previous to last Thursday who always opened the door and admitted visitors?"

"Yes, sir, except when he had his day off and then I did it."

"So it is quite possible that Miss Nina Fennel could have come to the house previous to last Thursday without your knowing it?"

"Yes, Sir."

Spike rose. "Thank you very much Emma, for your help. You don't mind if I look around a bit before I go?"

"Oh, no, sir," and she gave him a willing carte blanche to search the house.

"Just wait here a few moments for me," he said. "There may be one or two other things I've forgotten."

He bounded up the stairs two at a time until he was at the top of the landing on the second floor. Then quickly he started what was apparently a fruitless search. He went from room to room, sweeping each one with his glance—Thane's sitting room and bedroom, Cecily, Thane's apartment, and even the servants' rooms on the top floor. And when he returned to the first floor, he glanced in at the small bedroom-den at the back of the hall. In the drawing-room Emma was still waiting for him.

"If you don't mind," he said, "I'd like to take a look around downstairs too."

The basement floor laid out on the same plan as the other floors was divided into three rooms—the servants' sitting room in the front, a large butler's pantry that was a room in itself, and the kitchen in the back. Briefly his glance swept the three of them. And slowly a smile of dawning satisfaction seemed to light up his face. Then quickly he grew serious—very serious as he looked at the maid.

"And now, Emma," he said, "I want you to think very carefully. Very carefully, you understand."

Emma nodded and looked apprehensive.

"When Mr. Thane summoned you from your room last Monday night, you went directly down to Mrs. Thane's sitting room?"

"Yes, sir."

"And who was there?"

"Mr. Thane and—and—Mrs. Thane."

"And then what did you do?"

"Why Mr. Thane told me to run quick and get Dr. Partridge."

"And did you?"

"Yes, sir, you know that already."

"I suppose you didn't have time to dress?"

"No, sir, I just had on my kimono and slippers."

"And you went out the front door and next door to Dr Partridge's?"

"Yes, sir."

"Did you leave the door unlocked behind you?"

"Why, I don't know. I guess I must have."

"You didn't take a key with you?"

"No, I was too upset to think about a key."

"So, unless you had a key you couldn't have gotten back in—unless you left the door ajar behind you?"

"Yes, sir, that's right. We always keep the lock on."

"And you did get back in without any trouble?"

"Yes— No, wait a minute, let me see. No, I remember now. The door slammed to and I had to ring, and Mr. Thane came down and let us in."

Again the slow smile of dawning satisfaction lighted up Spike's face.

"Well, thanks very much again, Emma, for your help." At the door she stopped him. "Mr. Tracy—" She hesitated.

"Yes, Emma?"

"Isn't it true—about Mr. Fennel? I mean, didn't he do it?"

But Spike only smiled and slowly closed the door behind him. Once outside the Thane house he did not hesitate but went directly next door to Dr. Partridge and rang the bell. The doctor fortunately was in, sitting complacently in his shirt sleeves, with his toes comfortably wriggling in his stocking feet. As soon as his housekeeper announced the visitor, he hastily slipped on his shoes and became once more the bustling, slightly pompous person which be usually was when any one was about to observe him.

"Ah, Mr.—ah—"

"Tracy," Spike supplemented.

"Yes, Tracy. Sit down. Sit down. I've just been reading here," and he indicated the morning paper lying on the table, "the splendid work the police department has been doing. Splendid! Splendid!"

Spike smiled indulgently. "The difficulty is, though, Doctor, that it is only half done."

"Only half done? Why I understand that Mr. Fennel has confessed."

"Quite true. But the fact still remains that—" Spike paused as if uncertain quite how to proceed "Listen, Doctor, I need your help."

"Why, I'm sure, Mr. Tracy, that I have been at all times willing to do what I could and I still am, but I hardly see now—"

"I know. But just let me ask a few more questions."

The doctor nodded in assent and Spike went on, picking his words carefully and glancing up, now and again, to see just what effect they had on the little man.

"Tell me, Doctor, are you acquainted with Miss Nina Fennel?"

"No, I am not."

"Well then, do you know her father?"

"No. You must remember that outside of Mr. Thane, I know very little about the Thane household."

"I quite understand that. But did Mr. Thane ever speak to you about Mr. Fennel or his daughter, or any of the people involved in this case?"

The doctor thought carefully. "Well, once or twice he referred to Mr. Fennel but in an entirely casual way—just as he might refer to any other acquaintance. There was, I may say, on these occasions no suggestion of venom or animus in his attitude."

"Ever anything about the daughter?"

"No."

"Quite sure?"

"Quite sure."

"Strange," Spike mused. For a moment he sat thinking. Then he looked at the little doctor with his most engaging manner. "Dr Partridge, I am going to make a very strange request and I wish you would grant it without asking me just why I am making it."

"Well," the doctor temporized, "that depends, of course, on what it is."

"It's quite simple. I'm going to ask you to let me take a look at every room in your house. You may go along with me to make quite sure that I don't make away with the family plate. All I want is just to look."

"That seems easy enough," the doctor said indulgently. He rather liked this young man, and he was in a mood to humor him "Take as many looks as you like. Where shall we start?"

"Let's be systematic. How about beginning with the basement and going up?"

The doctor assented and led the way to the hall and down the flight of steps leading into the basement. The plan of the Partridge house was almost identical with that of the Thane house. For the second time that day Spike went from floor to floor, giving each room a minute but swift scrutiny—the kitchen and dining room in the basement, the doctor's sitting room and study on the first floor, the bedrooms on the second and third floors, and the servants' rooms on the top floor.

"Well," said the doctor when they had completed the search. "Did you find what you were looking for?"

"No," said Spike and grinned with great satisfaction.

But as they stood once more in the front hail of the first floor, he seemed loath to take his leave. It was as if something was still troubling him. Instead he went once more into the sitting room and sank into a chair with a somewhat weary sigh, and let his head rest on his hand.

"My dear fellow," the doctor, protested, "you're not ill, are you?"

Spike shook his head "No, I'm not ill. But this thing is rather getting on my nerves What I need just now is a good strong shot of liquor.'"

"Ah well, if that's all that's troubling you, just wait here a moment," and he disappeared into the hall and down the stairway to the basement.

As the sound of the doctor's slippers padding down the basement steps came to Spike, the weary droop seemed to melt from his shoulders and again the broad grin of satisfaction spread over his face. Quickly he reached for the doctor's coat and vest that lay over a near-by chair. But when the doctor returned not more than a minute later, he had resumed his crumpled, done-in attitude. With a grateful sigh, he sipped a glass of brandy and seemed visibly to brighten.

"Well, Doctor," he said at last, "thanks for your forbearance with the whims of youth. And thanks for the eye-opener. It certainly was."

And with a debonair twirl of his walking stick, Spike shut the door behind him and ran quickly down the steps of the house. There was no hesitation now in his movements. He hurried to the corner of Eighty-second Street and Columbus Avenue and hailed a taxi.

"Three Forty-six Hudson Street," he said. But on second thought he changed his mind. "No, just take me down around Times Square some place."

It was not until the early hours of Monday morning that he again hailed a cab and gave the Hudson Street address. The city room of the *New York Graphic* between the hours of twelve and four is a dreary place peopled only by grumbling charwomen struggling futilely with overflowing waste baskets, two or three tousled reporters pecking sleepily at typewriters, and a young man of serious mein sitting at the big horseshoe desk reading copy.

As Spike stood in the doorway surveying the room he had a sudden feeling of disappointment. For years when in New York he had been an assiduous reader of the highly colored tabloid, with its "thrill slayers," "torch murders," "gang wars," "love feuds" and assorted journalistic atrocities.

It hardly seemed possible that this highly seasoned fare could emanate from so commonplace a sanctum. *The Graphic* office he had always pictured as a ridiculous, mad, frenzied bedlam of rushing reporters; and instead he found it only a barn-like and very littered room, with the few sleepy inhabitants smoking and confiding to each other their secret dreams and longings.

Stifling his disappointment, he crossed to the serious young man at the copy desk and drew up a chair. The serious young man paused in the midst of the confessions of a bootlegger's mistress and looked up inquiringly.

"The name is Tracy," said Spike and tipped back his chair and settled his feet comfortably on the desk as he proffered a cigarette.

"Thanks," said the young man, "and what of it?"

"Oh, nothing. Nice name though, don't you think?"

"Yeah, but what the hell's that to me?"

"My dear fellow," Spike protested, "you should read the newspapers, really you should."

"Read the newspapers? Say, boy, I read the newspapers before they are newspapers," and he pointed impatiently to a pile of copy at his elbow that was waiting to be edited.

"Such is fame," and Spike sighed philosophically. "What I mean to say is, that it will be a terrible blow to my poor brother to realize how soon the world forgets."

"Say, lessen, what do you want, and spill it quick because I haven't got any time to fool."

"Very well." Spike immediately became businesslike and ceased his bantering. "I'm Spike Tracy, the brother of Richard Montgomery Tracy, the district attorney and I've been—ah—listening in on this Thane murder case."

The whole demeanor of the serious young man underwent a quick change. He pushed the pile of waiting copy aside and the impatient frown was supplanted by a look of keen curiosity, not unmixed with admiration.

"So you're the guy that's been throwing the monkey wrench into the works," he said.

"Well, of course, to the outsider it may seem that way. Personally, I've just been trying to be helpful."

"Just a regular little Pollyanna." The young man smiled for the first time "Of course," he explained quickly, "we don't dare tell the world that the Thane murder case was really brought to a successful conclusion by you. There are going to be other murders, and we wouldn't exactly like to get in bad with the Headquarters crowd by intimating that it took an amateur to show them up; but all the boys that are covering the case know."

"Stop—Stop—You'll have me chewing my thumb and looking flushed and coy."

"But really, the way you've solved this case is remarkable."

"But really, the case isn't solved."

"What do you mean?"

"I mean that it isn't solved."

"But Fennel's confessed—"

"My dear fellow," Spike looked at him indulgently, "you're almost as naïve as my brother and Inspector Herschman. You really should understand that in love and murder men always confess to scores of things that aren't true."

"But how do you know?"

"That's a long story. Too long to go into now."

"But if he didn't what's the idea of confessing?"

"Mr. Fennel has a very beautiful and hot-tempered daughter," Spike-said quietly.

"You mean—he's shielding her?"

"I don't mean anything just at present. I'm just groping around with a hazy idea in my mind about certain things. That's why I've come to you."

"Yeah?" There was a breathless note in his voice.

"Were you here in this office at four o'clock last Monday morning?"

"Yes."

"And, what happened just about that time?"

"Matthews called up and gave us the tip on the story. Charlie Matthews, the man that covers the Eighty-sixth Street Station."

"Just what did he say?"

"He was in an awful hurry. He just said to send some one up to 8 West Eighty-second Street immediately. A woman had been murdered."

"Anything else?"

"No. He hung up right away. He explained his hurry afterwards. He said that the cops weren't giving it out at the station and he just happened to overhear it. He knew that if he went himself they'd probably get sore and hold out stuff on him so he had me send up some one else."

"Matthews told you all this?"

"Yes."

"When?"

"The next night when I came on."

"Does Matthews ordinarily work in the daytime or the nighttime?"

"Daytime But he hangs around the station quite a bit at night too—just playing poker with some of the other fellows down there in the pressroom."

Spike frowned. It was apparent that this turn of events did not fit in with some slowly forming theory in his mind. He picked up a pencil from the desk and tapped it with an, irritated gesture against his teeth and finally brought his chair down with a bang.

"Are you sure it was Matthews you heard over the phone?"

"Of course it was. Why he got his $100 bonus the next day for it."

"What do you mean?"

"Well, every fellow that turns in a tip on what proves to be a big story gets a bonus if we beat the town on it."

"Oh, I see" Spike's frown melted into a smile. "Matthews doesn't happen by any chance to be around tonight does he?"

"His day off."

Spike rose slowly and stamped out his cigarette on the floor. "Thanks awfully. You've been very helpful."

"But say, lissen," the young man protested, "what's the new dope?"

"Nothing—yet. But if you see Mr. Matthews give him this card of mine and tell him if he wants to make another $100 to call around at my place at eight o'clock tomorrow morning."

XIX. A Tea Party at Police Headquarters

IT was Monday morning, almost a week after the murder of Cecily Thane. The district attorney of Kings County settled himself comfortably at his desk and rang for his secretary. He looked happier than he had for more than a week. The peculiar combination of depression and impatient irritability which had worn him down during the preceding week, seemed to have vanished completely. In his buttonhole was a scarlet spring flower, and on his face an expression of happy anticipation like one who having been disagreeably interrupted in a pleasing task, is suddenly released to pursue once more his pleasant way.

"The folder with the bank examiner's reports, Lovelace," he said, and took a deep breath of satisfaction as it was laid before him on the desk. Soon he was mulling happily through columns of figures and hefty tomes on financial jurisprudence. So engrossed was he in fact that he paid no attention to the leisurely entrance of his younger brother.

Spike as usual dropped into the nearest easy-chair and lit a cigarette. For a few moments he said nothing, but let his eyes rest in amused silence on his brother. At last by a slight movement he betrayed his presence, and Tracy looked up.

"Oh, hello," he said absently and reached for the latest report on the Fidelity Finance and Trust Corporation.

"Oh, hello," Spike responded lazily. "Still working on the Thane case?"

"The Thane case?" It was as if he were trying to search through his memory for a bit of ancient history. "No, thank Fortune, that's settled. Lovelace, please bring me Britt's Abstract of Laws Governing Bank Examiners in Great Britain."

For a few moments more he worked in silence, a pleased, zestful smile hovering about his lips. Spike sat and smoked in a leisurely fashion, his face now thoughtful, now over with a smile of satisfaction, now drawn into a puzzled frown. At last as if he had come to some conclusion, he broke his silence.

"I say, Richard, do you feel in an awfully benign, indulgent mood?"

"Eh—huh?" Only the surface of the district attorney's absorption was scratched and he went serenely ahead with his, work almost as if no one had spoken.

"I say, do you feel like humoring the whims of an erring but well-meaning brother?"

Tracy put down his pencil and looked over his glasses. "If it's money you want you can't have it. You've way overspent your allowance and you'll have to suffer."

"Richard, you have an absolutely putrid mind. You're always thinking that I'm thinking of either money or women."

"And I'm usually right."

"Usually, but in this instance you're all wet. I'm thinking of neither. I'm thinking of murder."

"Still thinking, I see, that you know more about the Thane murder than we do."

"I'm not thinking I know more about it. I do."

"Do you know, Philip Tracy, your conceit is appalling?"

"I haven't a doubt of it, brother. It is equaled only by my charm and perspicacity."

"Well, I'm very sorry, but I haven't the time to argue the matter with you this morning. I'm busy."

"Not half as busy as you're going to be."

"Now listen here, Philip, please go away and don't bother me. I've a great many things to do to get this report in shape for the next meeting of the Bar Association and I can't—"

"Can it, dearie, can it." And Spike reached forth a lazy hand and pressed the buzzer at the corner of the desk.

"Lovelace," he said, when the secretary, appeared, "would you ask Inspector Herschman to be so kind as to step this way?"

When the secretary had left, the district attorney laid down his pencil with an exasperated frown. "Well, go ahead. What crazy idea have you thought up now?"

"Crazy is right. It's so utterly fantastic that I can hardly believe it myself."

In a few minutes Herschman strode into the room. Like the district attorney he too seemed to have just emerged triumphantly from a trying experience,, and to have been restored once more to the favor of the gods. He was smiling broadly —even when his glance encountered Spike.

"My brother here," said Tracy with the deprecating gesture which he used when referring to Spike, "insists that he has something to add to the Thane murder case."

Herschman grinned. "With Fennel's signed confession in our hands, I don't think there's much to add."

But Spike was not at all daunted by the unfriendly reception. He offered Herschman a cigarette, held a light for him and even smiled benignly while doing it.

"Well, seeing as how you two are all frothing at the mouth with impatience and enthusiasm. I'll come right down to the point. I'm going out for a bit and while I'm gone, I want you to get Nina Fennel, Elton Thane, Emma, Tommy Spencer, Dr. Partridge and George Griffis down here in this office. Get them all here and hold 'em until I get back from where I'm going."

"Come now, Philip, you're being ridiculous."

"Perhaps," Spike admitted. "And then again I may be being tremendously clever. Just at present I don't know myself."

"What's the idea?"

"The idea, Inspector, is so wild, crazy that I haven't the heart to tell even you until. I'm a bit more sure. All I want to know is will you or won't you?"

"Certainly not," Tracy said emphatically.

"Oh, very well, then." Spike shrugged his shoulders and reached for his stick and hat. "It will be frightfully embarrassing for you two, though, when I write my confessions as an amateur detective for the *Graphic* and call attention to the fact that you are about to send the wrong person to the electric chair."

"Wrong person? What do you mean?"

"I mean, old thing, that Mortimer Fennel did not kill Cecily Thane. Well, au revoir. I'll send you marked copies of the paper."

But he got no further than the door.

"Stop!" The district attorney's voice had an uneasy edge to it. "Where are you going?"

"I think I'll go up to Columbia and register for a course in journalism to prepare me for my career as a writer."

"Come back and sit down."

For a moment Spike hesitated. Then with a leisurely air he re-crossed the room and sank into the chair he had just vacated.

"Inspector Herschman," Tracy pointed out, "who was tracking criminals when you were still crying for your bottle, has gone very thoroughly into Mortimer Fennel's confession. and has assured me that we will not have the slightest difficulty getting a conviction for first degree murder on it."

"Oh, quite. I haven't a doubt of it. But I was under the impression—please correct me if I am wrong—that the highest standards of the legal profession demanded justice rather than convictions."

With an exasperated sigh of surrender the district attorney pushed aside the papers on which he had been working. "All right, go ahead. What have you been doing now?" His tone was very much that of a mother who strongly suspects that Willie has broken a window or made a forbidden raid on the pantry. "What makes you say that Mortimer Fennel did not kill Cecily Thane?"

"Well, Sunday morning I went over to the prison ward of the hospital and talked to him. No, perhaps that isn't entirely correct. He's too weak for sustained conversation. I asked him just one question. The answer he gave me convinced me that as far as murdering goes he's still a bum commercial artist."

"And what was the question?"

"I asked him where Cecily Thane was standing when he shot her and he said in front of the safe. If you're not too weary to rack your brains, you'll remember that a very revealing little bullet hole was found in the chaise longue."

"He was delirious," Herschman put in sharply.

"No, he wasn't delirious. His brain was perfectly clear and his temperature was normal. I asked the nurse."

The inspector and the district attorney eyed each other uneasily in silence and Spike watched a hurdy-gurdy man who was grinding away on the sidewalk below.

"Well, gentlemen," he said finally, "will you or won't you?"

"Will we or won't we what?"

"Ask Nina Fennel, Elton Thane, Emma, Tommy Spencer—write 'em down so you won't forget 'em—Dr. Partridge and George Griffis to drop in this afternoon and have a dish o' tea with you, and then hold 'em here until I get back? My own contribution to the gathering will be Mr. Charlie Matthews of the *Evening Graphic*, one of the greatest little opportunists I know."

Again the district attorney and the inspector exchanged glances. "Oh, all right, all right," Tracy finally gave in in an exasperated voice. With an irritated gesture he pressed the buzzer for his secretary and indicated the papers in front of him. "Lovelace," be snapped, "gather these up and put them back in my working file."

When Spike walked into the district attorney's office two hours later his brother and Inspector Herschman were making a valiant but unsuccessful attempt to conceal from their six guests the feeling that something was up. One glance at the satisfied air with which Spike stood in the doorway and surveyed the room convinced the uncomfortable hosts that whatever had been his errand, it had been successful.

Despite all elaborate efforts to be casual, there was a certain excitement in the air. George Griffis and Elton Thane, disregarding the differences which had come between them in the past, were sitting close together as if for mutual protection, and occasionally they exchanged a low-voiced remark.

Dr. Partridge was like a nervous, curious little bird, mystified but rather enjoying the situation. Charlie Matthews, a young fellow of engaging appearance and exceedingly rumpled clothes, in the best reportorial traditions, was alert and waiting for whatever might break. And Emma, the maid, sat in one corner obviously frightened.

Nina Fennel was by herself, a little apart from the others, scarcely ever looking at them, her hands listless in her lap. Only her eyes which rested with tragic intensity on the Tombs across the way, gave a hint of what was going on in her mind. And directly across the room from her was Tommy Spencer, looking at her with an expression in which apprehension was mingled with an almost touching wistfulness.

Of the ten people in the room, Spike alone seemed untouched by the general atmosphere of tense expectancy. With his usual airy greeting he addressed them collectively and proceeded in a leisurely manner to lay aside his hat and stick, and draw out his cigarette case. But for once he did not slouch down into the nearest easy-chair. Instead he stood before them slightly in the manner of a guest at a house party about to do card tricks.

"Frightfully good of you all to come down," he assured them in a tone which was designed to put them at their ease but which failed dismally of its purpose. "I hope I haven't inconvenienced you any."

But as no one either protested or affirmed he went ahead. "The fact is that we've discovered who murdered Cecily Thane, and as you all are more or less interested—or perhaps I should say involved, I thought you might be curious to hear about it."

Out of the corner of his eye, he cast a glance at the district attorney and the inspector sitting to the side of the group, and finding them both slightly pop-eyed, he smiled.

"My brother and Inspector Herschman here, have not been satisfied with the confession of Mr. Mortimer Fennel. They have felt all along that Mr. Fennel in assuming the guilt was acting from a motive which although noble was slightly misguided. It is only natural, of course, that a father should strive to protect a daughter."

He paused. Nina Fennel's eyes suddenly tore themselves away from the Tombs. It was difficult to tell whether the glance she shot at the young man before her was one of frantic question or pure terror. Quickly she pressed the back of her hand across her mouth as if to stifle a word—a cry. But Spike only smiled benignly in her direction much in the manner of a Sunday-school superintendent addressing the primary class, and went on.

"Mr. George Griffis' possession of at least one of the pieces of jewelry missing from the safe has seemed an incontrovertible bit of evidence in refutation of Mr. Fennel's confession."

Again he paused and the eyes of every one in the room focused on Griffis He sat stiff, immobile, his glance shifting nervously from the toes of his shoes to a far corner of the room, to the side, back to his shoes, but never once meeting the gaze of any of the other nine people.

"The case, you see," Spike went on, "has many mystifying aspects. Perhaps not the least of these is Mr. Tommy Spencer. Gentlemen—and ladies—" here he bowed to Nina Fennel and Emma, "I offer as exhibit A in this puzzling situation Tommy's frank and open face."

But at the moment Tommy's face failed dismally to fit the description. Like Griffis his glance was shifting from one side to the other and his fingers toyed nervously with the watch chain across the front of his vest.

"Not, I will admit, a very convincing performance," Spike remarked, "but nevertheless I offer him in evidence. Evidence of the amazing difficulties which gentlemen of his sort are likely to encounter in the peculiar type of business by which they earn their living.

"Gentlemen, and ladies, let me introduce—the goat. Tommy has been so unfortunate as to embrace a profession which seems to be characterized by a high and spectacular mortality rate among the clientele. You all remember the Schlockenhass case. Tommy, as you are doubtless aware, was the gentleman who was known to have been the last person to see Greta Schlockenbass alive. And he is also the last person who is known to have seen Cecily Thane alive. The coincidence is rather striking, don't you think?"

Spike looked around with a bright inquiring glance.

Then suddenly and for the first time that afternoon his demeanor underwent a quick change. No longer was he the parlor entertainer. His face became set into grave lines and his voice lost its note of levity. He stood now perfectly still, his arms folded in front of him.

"The person who killed Cecily Thane deliberately framed the crime on Tommy Spencer. Knowing Tommy's previous connection with the Schlockenhass case, knowing his ill-repute with the police, the guilty person laid careful plans to throw the blame upon him. The plan as executed was one of clock-like precision, timed to the minute.

"In less than five minutes after Tommy Spencer left the Thane house last Monday night, the guilty person shot Cecily Thane through the heart as she lay on the chaise longue, dragged her body across the floor, placed it in front of the safe, picked up the bullet which had gone through the back of the chaise longue and drove it into the wall of the bedroom, giving the impression that she was shot as she stood in front of the wall safe. To complete further the illusion of robbery the safe was rifled."

Spike paused and there was a deathly tense silence in the room. Not a soul moved—breathed.

"The murderer knew that Tommy Spencer would be suspected immediately. The murderer believed that as soon as Tommy learned of the murder of Cecily Thane he would realize his own peril and disappear.

"It was necessary, therefore, that Tommy should learn the news as soon as possible. So the guilty person took the one sure way to do it. The murderer telephoned the *New York Evening Graphic* the story. And then to make sure that Tommy would have plenty of time to get away in, the murderer removed from Cecily Thane's telephone directory the S page containing his number, so that, the police would have to spend at least five or six hours locating his apartment."

Spike paused again and his eyes swept his audience. Nina Fennel still sat with the back of her hand pressed convulsively against her trembling lips. George Griffis gnawed at his knuckles. Elton Thane nervously wiped his mouth with his handkerchief.

All of them were staring straight at Spike now as if hypnotized by his unfolding of the murder plot. Then slowly the eyes of one of the nine people before him wavered, glazed, grew wide and agonized and a gasping, tortured voice spoke.

"He's— He's right—I—I killed her—I did—just what he said—I—"

With a sudden rasping moan, Elton Thane pitched forward, face down on to the floor. His body jerked convulsively and then was still.

For a moment no one moved. They stood, transfixed by the sight before them. Dr. Partridge was the first to recover himself. He sprang forward, turned the prostrate man upon his back. Quickly his hand sought the pulse. He listened. Then he laid the hand down.

"Dead!?"

The ghastly quiet of the room was broken only by the hysterical weeping of Nina Fennel. "Tommy—my father—didn't—Tommy!"

XX. Spike Borrows $5,000

SPIKE woke from a deep, dreamless, twelve-hour sleep. Slowly, lazily he stretched and then lay still, enjoying to the full that first delicious drowsiness that immediately follows sleep. Presently he reached out a hand to the bedside table and fumbled in a small leather box for a cigarette, lit it and lay back against the pillows, puffing contentedly.

"Your brother and another gentleman to see you sir." It was Meeks, the servant, who stood in the half-opened doorway leading to the sitting room. "They've been here twice before this morning, but I told them you left word you were not to be disturbed."

Spike smiled. "The Mountain comes to Mahomet. The combined legal and police minds of New York County sit patiently on my doorstep."

"Yes, sir."

"Well, show them in."

As Montgomery Tracy and Inspector Herschman entered the room there was in their attitude toward the man in the bed a suggestion almost of awe and respect. The district attorney attempted to smile, and the inspector fumbled with his hat. Spike apparently was the only one completely at his ease and he was very much so.

"Meeks, a couple of drinks for the gentlemen, and one for me. And have one yourself, Meeks. I feel particularly set up this morning."

Tracy and Herschman seated themselves.

"Well?" said the district attorney, but this time there was none of that peremptory irritation which usually characterized the word when he addressed it to his brother. It was rather as if he were discreetly suggesting that if it were not too much trouble, would Spike mind beginning.

"Yeah," supplemented Herschman, "go ahead. Spill it."

"But first, Inspector," said Spike, "tell me if I was right."

"Oh, you were right, all right. Everything checks exactly."

"And Thane?"

"Strychnine sulphate tablets. We found a box of them in his pocket. Partridge says be must have taken about three grains, it acted so quick."

"Any trace of the jewels?"

"Up in Thane's room, hid in some old books that he had taken the stuffing out of."

"I didn't imagine that a man of Thane's close nature could bear to chuck $150,000 worth of Jewelry into the river. He'd probably planned to cut up the larger and more distinctive stones later on and use them in his business. How about the gun?"

"Not a sign of it."

"All guns missing—Tommy's, Nina Fennel's, Elton Thane's. Really, you know, if I'm ever suspected of murder I shan't make the mistake of egging on the police by chucking mine away. And how is Miss Fennel?"

"Oh, she's all right. She's been over to the hospital most of the time with her father. They've moved him into a private ward and he's coming along O.K. But say, lissen, young fel— Mr. Tracy—"

"Inspector, spare me. After all we've been through together, just make it Spike."

"Well, what I mean is, we want to know all the dope. You—you pulled a pretty neat job—and—" Herschman fumbled He was not used to his new role and his lines were halting. "I got to hand it to you. And if I've said anything in the past that—well—"

"Quite," said Spike magnanimously. "I understand perfectly, Inspector. How were you to know that Richard's impression of me was false. A most natural error, which only adds to your human, lovable qualities."

The inspector looked slightly bewildered but relieved. He was not used to being called 'lovable" but he was glad to be spared putting his apology into words.

Meeks entered with three frost-clouded glasses. Spike lifted his toward his two guests. "Yours for bigger and better murders!"

He and the inspector each took a big gulp, but the district attorney only sipped his. The toast was apparently not to his liking.

"Now Philip," he said, "we are most curious to know how you arrived at your conclusion that it was Elton Thane who murdered Cecily Thane. I may say that I join with Inspector Herschman in a sincere—ah—regret that I have at times been not wholly confident of your abilities. You have, I may point rendered me a great service."

From his inside pocket he drew forth a newspaper clipping with a morning date line on it. It was from the same paper which less than a fortnight before had been calling the district attorney to task for his failure as a criminal investigator. The editorial read:

"It is apparent that District Attorney Tracy and his aides in the police department have turned over a new leaf. The dispatch with which they have handled the Thane murder case will do much toward re-establishing the confidence of the people of New York in their administration. Confronted with a difficult criminal tangle of many muddled and misleading aspects, the issue clouded by a false confession, they brought the guilty man to justice and saved an Innocent man from the electric chair. They are to be congratulated."

Spike handed the clipping back to his brother and smiled.

"And I may say," the district attorney began, "that I am grateful to you, that is—your modesty—ah—I feel most uncomfortable at receiving credit which by right— ah—"

"Quite!" Spike interrupted. "Credit for having made a few pertinent suggestions as to the murderer of Cecily

Thane will be of no use whatever to me in my subsequent career of debauchery and light living. But you can use it quite neatly and you're welcome to it." He waved his hand in magnanimous dismissal of the subject.

"Well, go on," Herschman urged with impatient curiosity. "Shoot the works. What tipped you off to the fact that Thane, himself, was the guy."

"Well, Inspector, if you would be a more assiduous reader of detective stories you would realize that it is always the person with the iron-clad alibi who is the guilty one—the person who apparently couldn't possibly have been there to do the dirty work. And in this case that person was Thane."

"Tommy, Nina Fennel, Mortimer Fennel, George Griffis, all of them quite possibly could have been there. Tommy easily enough Nina Fennel and Mortimer Fennel just as easy. Emma you remember saw neither of them leave. They said they left at nine and nine-thirty, but did they? One or the other or both of them might easily have hidden in the house, waited until Cecily Thane returned and Tommy left."

"Well, I never thought of the girl and her father working together," Herschman said. "I thought there was something between her and Spencer."

"I rather imagine that there was something between them. Nina Fennel probably planned months in advance to use Tommy Spencer in some way to break Mrs. Thane's hold on her father. Just how, I don't believe she knew. Actual murder I'm sure she never contemplated. And then on that Monday afternoon when Cecily Thane finally made good her threat and sent a letter to Mrs. Fennel she and her father both went all blah.

"The father particularly. As he explained in his 'confession' he's been pretty much of a clinging vine to that Amazonian daughter of his. They went to the Thane house to appeal directly to Mrs. Thane. Then both of them lost their heads and wandered about aimlessly.

"Finally Nina went down to Spencer's apartment and wrote what turned out later to be a most incriminating note. But how was she to know that the police would interpret the 'terrible thing' that she mentioned to mean the murder of Mrs. Thane. At any rate, that was the way Tommy Spencer interpreted it. He has thought all along that she did it, and he's cringed every time her name was mentioned in connection with the case. What she really meant, of course, was the letter sent to her mother."

"But since she was innocent and knew she was, why in hell throw away that gun the next day?" Herschman persisted.

"Certainly she knew she was innocent, but all she knew about her father was that he did not come home the previous night until after one o'clock. And she probably jumped to the conclusion that in his desperation he did it."

"But why didn't he tell her he didn't?"

"Because, my dear fellow, he was thinking just the same thing about her. And when two people begin thinking things like that about each other, they usually end up by making damn fools of themselves.

"She threw the gun away because she was afraid the police would find it and suspect her father. And he confessed because he thought she had done it, and he was having a delayed attack of nobility. Each one was trying to shield the other."

"What about George Griffis. How did he get one of the missing pieces of jewelry?"

"He probably just lifted it when he went to see his sister Monday afternoon—"

"Then why did Thane include it in the list of things he gave me?"

"If you'll think back you'll realize that up to the time that he gave you that list he didn't have much time to take stock. He probably stuffed the jewels into their hiding place immediately after he shot his wife. Then he hurried directly to Dr. Partridge's. He had no time to look the stuff over when he came back to the house to 'discover' his wife's dead body. Five minutes later Partridge arrived and was with him constantly until we saw him the next morning.

"In all that time he had really no opportunity that he dared risk to take an invoice. It was not until after he had given you the description that he was alone long enough to look over the swag and realize his mistake. As the piece which Griffis took was one of the most spectacular and distinctive, he simply jumped to the conclusion that of course it was in the lot that he had removed from the safe.

"Griffis, for his part, was scared, of course, of grand larceny. What probably happened was—when he found out that he wasn't going to get any money out of his sister, he simply waited for a moment when her back was turned, and then picked up the nearest bit of pawnable stuff that happened to be handy. And, by the way, did the forged check come to light anywhere?"

"Yes," Herschman answered, "we located the bank where she kept a private lock box under another name. That check was the only damn thing in it."

"Probably the most lucrative investment she had," Spike pointed out.

"But you're still not telling us," the inspector persisted "how Thane could have been in two places at once. The maid swore that it was just twelve o'clock when Spencer left and Partridge swore that it was ten minutes of twelve when he arrived at his house where he stayed until four. So how could he have been in his own house at twelve and shot his wife?"

"If you'll just lend me your pencil and fetch me a piece of paper from that writing desk I'll draw a picture of it."

But the picture which he drew was not a floor plan of the Thane and Partridge houses. It was merely a series of crossing lines filled in with figures, with a few notes written at the side. When he had finished it he handed it to the two men.

"I think from the very start I suspected Thane, but it was just one of those groundless sort of feelings which all the evidence seemed to refute. How could he have been in his own house at twelve o'clock or shortly after and shot his wife when all the time he was in another place?

"And it was just one of those little inconsequential things that we didn't pay much attention to at the time that kept aggravating my belief in the apparently impossible. You'll remember that the fingerprint pictures showed that the knob of the wall safe had been wiped clean.

"Thane was firm in his statement that only he and his wife knew the combination. If she opened the safe, as the circumstances seemed to indicate, why did the murderer take the trouble to wipe her fingerprints off the knob? Especially in view of the fact that the whole thing was staged to give the impression that she had opened the safe and had been shot the second afterward.

"The only other person who knew the combination was Thane. And if he opened it, naturally, he wouldn't want to be leaving his print around. The logical thing for him to do would be to wipe it off. Am I right?"

Herschman nodded in agreement. "Yeah, that's sense."

"After I talked to Miss Audrey Keating that certain feeling increased. Here was a perfectly sound motive for Thane. He wanted to marry another woman. And his wife wouldn't divorce him. And when he tried to force her into it, and God knows he had enough evidence with Mortimer Fennel at hand, she probably pulled that forged check on him and dared him to go ahead and start action. Her death was for him the only solution.

"But then I didn't have another thing to go on—just a hunch, and a theory, and one insignificant piece of evidence. Until—" Spike paused and turned a reproving gaze upon his brother.

"I think, Richard," he went on, "that my very first attempt to be helpful in this case was dismissed by you as facetious. When I suggested the very first morning as we mounted the steps of the Thane house, that we stop and have a little chat with the workmen in the excavation in front, you reminded me that there was a time and a place for levity.

"As a matter of fact it was one of those workmen that set me on the right track. You remember that Emma testified that she heard no sound of a shot after she let Tommy Spencer out of the door and added something of this sort—'but heaven knows that's not to be wondered at with all that racket going on outside.'

"However, my little chat with the foreman who was working there the eventful Monday night revealed the fact that the racket stopped that night promptly at twelve, when the automatic shift bell rang and the shifts changed.

"So it's reasonable to believe, isn't it, that if the shot had been fired after twelve when there was no noise outside to drown it out, Emma would have heard it."

He paused and looked inquiringly at his audience.

"Yeah, that's right," Herschman said. "Even if the shooting was done with the door to the sitting room closed, there's a pretty, clean sweep of sound from the second floor to the basement."

"Well then," Spike went on, "I decided that the shot must have been fired before twelve o'clock."

"While Spencer was still there?"

"No, after he left."

"But he didn't leave until twelve. You remember how hard the maid stuck to that point. She swore that it was almost exactly twelve by her clock in the basement when she let him out."

"And so it was—by her clock. But the right time was really ten minutes of twelve."

"I don't get you."

"It's really quite easy when you look at the diagram. But wait! Let me explain what I did after I talked to the workman. It was really he that gave me the idea that perhaps the time played a bigger part in this than we had suspected.

"You will recall that almost every one who came in contact with Elton Thane that night for some reason or other remembered the exact time. The clerk in the drug store on the corner of Columbus Avenue and Seventy-sixth Street. Naturally enough, to be sure. It was his last half hour and of course he was clock watching.

"But to make doubly sure that the clerk would remember him, Thane bought five boxes of very expensive cigars. Five boxes. He would have bought six if the store had had them. And both Tommy Spencer and Dr. Partridge hinted at the fact that Thane was notoriously tight with money. One box would have been sufficient as a gift. But five fixed him more clearly in the clerk's mind.

"And because Thane was late to his appointment with Partridge, the good doctor naturally drew out his watch and looked at the time and upbraided him—and remembered therefore that it was ten minutes to twelve, exactly, when Thane arrived."

"Yeah, and where does that leave you?" Herschman protested.

"It would leave us still high and dry, had I not lowered myself to lawful larceny." Spike paused and grinned.

"What do you mean?"

"Well, if I tell you, will you promise that nothing I say will be used against me?"

"Sure, go ahead."

"Well, to get back to my break with the workmen. When I left off talking to them, I went into the Thane house and had another chat with Emma. I was rather afraid she would suspect what I had on my mind, so I threw in a lot of misleading questions about Thane's quarrel with the butler and whether she had ever seen Nina Fennel and gave the impression that I was hot on the young lady's trail. My real object was to search the Thane house thoroughly for just one thing—clocks."

"Yeah, clocks. What's the idea?" Herschman was sitting on the edge of his chair now tense with excitement.

"The idea is that I found only one clock in the entire house. The alarm clock which the servants keep down in the servants' sitting room and carry up to the top floor with them at night. Not another clock in the whole place.

"At Dr. Partridge's I went through the same rigmarole and found several. One on the basement floor in the kitchen. One in the housekeeper's room on the third floor. None in the rooms in which he lives on the first and second floors.

"The doctor, I should point out, was, most fortunately for me, in his shirt sleeves when I arrived. He had laid his vest and coat across a chair in the sitting room—even as he did the night that Cecily Thane was murdered. So I summoned up all the dramatic talent I could, faked a great weariness and asked little Peregrine for a drink. He went down to the basement to get the decanter of wine— the very same decanter that he had fetched up the night Elton Thane played chess with him. And while he was gone I swiped his watch."

Spike paused and grinned "Remember," he reminded them, "that I have your word that you'll not send me up the river."

"But what was the idea" Herschman was still puzzled.

"The idea was that by this time I had a wild crazy notion in my head and I wanted to verify it. I'll admit I was slightly, dramatic—melodramatic, if you will. I took a chance on being right. I went down to Headquarters and had you two assemble the gang. And while you were rounding them up I went up to Elton Thane's branch store on Broadway at Eighty-seventh Street and waited around a bit until I was sure that he wasn't in the place— that he was on his way down to meet you two.

"Then I went in and pulled out Partridge's watch, pretended that it was my own and raised hell because it hadn't been keeping good time. Just as I suspected, the

Thane establishment like every well-run jewelry place keeps a careful record of each watch that is brought in for regulation or repair. A sort of case history. I had them look up my watch and found that the truth was even as I had suspected."

Spike paused, tantalizing

"Yeah?" Herschman could hardly contain his curiosity. "Go ahead. What did the jewelry shop records show?"

"They showed that on May 15, the day Cecily Thane was murdered, Dr. Partridge's watch was taken from the shop by Elton Thane himself, and delivered to Dr. Partridge."

"And on the way home, Thane set it back," Herschman broke in.

"Exactly."

"Well now, who would have thought of that?"

"Elton Thane, I imagine, had thought about every detail for quite a long time," Spike went on. "May 15 was probably the culmination of months of planning. And then suddenly everything resolved itself into his hands. Dr. Partridge turned his watch in to be fixed and it was an easy enough matter for Thane to hold it until a night when he knew his wife was to be out with Spencer. And then fortune played right into his hands, gave him an advantage he had scarcely hoped for. Spencer reported that he would be home early that night.

"From then on things were easy. You remember that Emma said that Thane sent her out about eight o'clock to post a letter. While she was gone he probably turned her clock downstairs forward ten minutes. Partridge's was already turned back ten minutes. That means that he had twenty minutes' leeway. The rest is easy if you just look at the diagram."

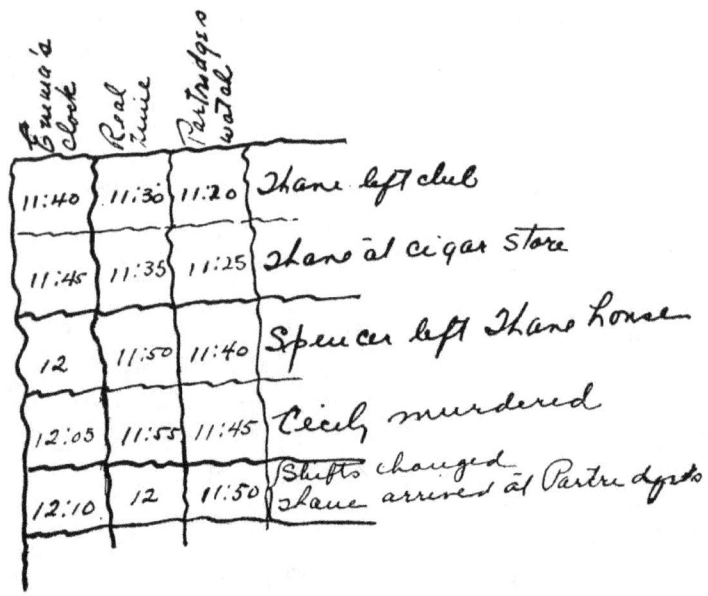

Emma's clock	Real time	Partridge's watch	
11:40	11:30	11:20	Thane left club
11:45	11:35	11:25	Thane at cigar store
12	11:50	11:40	Spencer left Thane house
12:05	11:55	11:45	Cecily murdered
12:10	12	11:50	Shifts changed. Thane arrived at Partridge's

The three men bent their heads over the hasty pencil chart that Spike had just made and he explained as he went along.

"When Spencer left the house, Thane was probably watching from some vantage point near by. When the coast was clear he slipped into the house, went up to his wife's room and shot her while the drilling machines in the subway excavation were still making a terrific racket Then he went down immediately and went next door to Dr. Partridge's, arriving there, according to the doctor's watch, at ten minutes of twelve. Actually, of course, it was just twelve. Neat, eh?"

Spike laid down the pencil and leaned back against the pillows. The district attorney and the inspector were silent, but it was the silence of admiration, of tribute.

"Well, I got to hand it to him," Herschman said finally. "The kid's clever."

"Don't be so ambiguous, Inspector. Who are you referring to—Elton Thane or me?"

"Aw—you know I mean you."

"Well, it goes for Thane, too. He had every detail planned carefully ahead of time. Take the cutting of the telephone wire."

"Yeah, what the hell did he do that for? His wife couldn't put in a call after he'd shot her."

"Of course not. It was just his way of playing for a most necessary bit of time. It's quite plain that if his alibi was to be any good, the watch and the clock which he had tampered with would have to be set back or forward again to the right time."

The inspector nodded in agreement.

"Very well then, Thane just trusted to pure blind luck and the mildness of the night that Partridge would take off his vest with his watch in it. And luck was with him. Knowing where Partridge kept his decanter, he probably suggested a drink and Partridge went downstairs to get it. While he was gone Thane turned the watch forward to the correct time.

"Then his problem was to turn Emma's clock back ten minutes. And so when he returned to his own house and aroused her, he told her to summon Partridge, by telephone. When the telephone wouldn't work, it was quite the natural thing to assume that all the telephones in the house were out of order and he told her to foot it. That left him with time to do two very important things. Go up to her room and set her clock back, and put in a call to the *Graphic* from the telephone downstairs."

"Yeah, but why didn't the paper get hep? I should think that a tip like that with nothing to explain it would get them going."

"Of course. And there again Thane played into luck. I don't imagine he was personally acquainted with Mr. Charles Matthews. But fortunately for him Mr. Matthews is not above taking money which in the strictest sense of the term he has not earned. In view of the fact that the paper offers a $100 bonus to a reporter who turns in an exclusive tip, far be it from Charlie to inform the hand that signs the checks that he had nothing to do with the call which caused the *Graphic* to beat the town on Tuesday morning.

"You see, up to this point every one concerned played right into his hands. But he hadn't counted on the visit of Mortimer Fennel. You'll remember that not until after he talked with us on Tuesday morning did he have a chance to talk to Emma. And when he learned that Fennel had been there, he probably threw the fear of God into her and told her not to be so gabby with policemen. Naturally he didn't want Fennel drawn into the case. People might think he had killed his wife because she was unfaithful. He hadn't an idea, of course, that we'd ever even know of the existence of Miss Audrey Keating. She—"

Suddenly, for no reason at all, Spike grew pensive, slightly appealing as he looked at his brother.

"Richard, my boy," he began tentatively, "I don't suppose you could lend me some money?"

Tracy stiffened. The admiring mood vanished.

"How much and what for?"

"Quite a lot and if I were to tell you what for you'd look even more sour than you do already."

"A woman, as usual."

"Simply a mind reader you are, Richard. Simply a mind reader."

"Let me remind you, Philip, as I have many times before, that I will not lend myself to—"

"Before you go on, old thing, would you mind letting me read that editorial from this morning's paper over again—out loud?"

For a moment the two brothers looked at each other. Then slowly the eyes of the older fell. "About five thousand," said Spike and Tracy reached for his check book.

"Thanks awfully," he said when at last he held the still inky check.

Suddenly Herschman broke into a hearty, paternal laugh. "Go to it, boy! But tell the gal the next time she's mixed up in a murder case to hang on to her gun."

Spike turned a questioning glance on the inspector.

"Nina Fennel, ain't it?" "Herschman went on. "I could see you fell hard the first very day."

"Oh, my word no, Inspector. You know I've decided that there is no such thing as a perfect blue-eyed brunette. They either have husbands or else they, have strong, noble characters which is even worse. As a matter of fact I was wrong about Nina Fennel, or at least partly wrong."

"What do you mean?"

"Well, I think I was quite correct in thinking that she originally took up with Tommy because she intended to use him. And then after she got to know him—well—" Spike made a gesture to indicate the utter simplicity of the whole thing.

"She's a strong-minded sort of person who has to have some one around her who's leaning and depending. She's just the sort to fall for a weak but appealing chap like Tommy. He took her home from the bit of melodrama we staged yesterday at Headquarters, and from the ecstatic letter which I got from him this morning, I have a feeling that Nina has consented to lead him on to a higher and nobler life. He says he has definitely abandoned his precarious profession." Spike paused and threw off the covers and stepped out of bed.

"No, no, inspector! I'm sorry to destroy your little idyl of dreams and romance, but I've decided to go in for blondes from now on—Middle Western blondes who try to talk like Lady Oxford's drawing-room."

THE END

Resurrected Press Books in *The Chief Inspector Pointer Mystery* Series

RESURRECTED PRESS BOOKS IN H. ASHBOOK'S
DETECTIVE SPIKE TRACY MYSTERY SERIES

The Murder of Cicely Thane (1930)

The Murder of Stephen Kester (1931)

The Murder of Sigurd Sharon (1933)

A Most Immoral Murder (1935)

Murder Makes Murder (1937)

Murder Comes Back (1940)

Murder on Friday (1941)

RESURRECTED PRESS BOOKS FROM *THE ETHEL THOMAS DETECTIVE STORY* SERIES BY CORTLAND FITZSIMMON'S

The Whispering Window

The Moving Finger

Mystery at Hidden Harbor

The Evil Men Do

RESURRECTED PRESS BOOKS FROM *THE JAMES "BONNIE" DUNDEE MYSTERY* SERIES BY ANNE AUSTIN

The Black Pigeon

The Avenging Parrot

Murder Backstairs

Murder at Bridge

One Drop of Blood

Murdered, But Not Dead

AVAILABLE FROM RESURRECTED PRESS!

THE EDWARDIAN DETECTIVES
LITERARY SLEUTHS OF THE EDWARDIAN ERA

The exploits of the great Victorian Detectives, Poe's C. Auguste Dupin, Gaboriau's Lecoq, and most famously, Arthur Conan Doyle's Sherlock Holmes, are well known. But what of those fictional detectives that came after, those of the Edwardian Age? The period between the death of Queen Victoria and the First World War had been called the Golden Age of the detective short story, but how familiar is the modern reader with the sleuths of this era? And such an extraordinary group they were, including in their numbers an unassuming English priest, a blind man, a master of disguises, a lecturer in medical jurisprudence, a noble woman working for Scotland Yard, and a savant so brilliant he was known as "The Thinking Machine."

To introduce readers to these detectives, Resurrected Press has assembled a collection of stories featuring these and other remarkable sleuths in The Edwardian Detectives.

- The Case of Laker, Absconded by Arthur Morrison
- The Fenchurch Street Mystery by Baroness Orczy
- The Crime of the French Café by Nick Carter
- The Man with Nailed Shoes by R Austin Freeman
- The Blue Cross by G. K. Chesterton
- The Case of the Pocket Diary Found in the Snow by Augusta Groner
- The Ninescore Mystery by Baroness Orczy
- The Riddle of the Ninth Finger by Thomas W. Hanshew
- The Knight's Cross Signal Problem by Ernest Bramah

- The Problem of Cell 13 by Jacques Futrelle
- The Conundrum of the Golf Links by Percy James Brebner
- The Silkworms of Florence by Clifford Ashdown
- The Gateway of the Monster by William Hope Hodgson
- The Affair at the Semiramis Hotel by A. E. W. Mason
- The Affair of the Avalanche Bicycle & Tyre Co., LTD by Arthur Morrison

RESURRECTED PRESS CLASSIC MYSTERY CATALOGUE

Journeys into Mystery
Travel and Mystery in a More Elegant Time

The Edwardian Detectives
Literary Sleuths of the Edwardian Era

Gems of Mystery
Lost Jewels from a More Elegant Age

E. C. Bentley
Trent's Last Case: The Woman in Black

Ernest Bramah
Max Carrados Resurrected:
The Detective Stories of Max Carrados

Agatha Christie
The Secret Adversary
The Mysterious Affair at Styles

Octavus Roy Cohen
Midnight

Freeman Wills Croft
The Ponson Case
The Pit Prop Syndicate

J. S. Fletcher
The Herapath Property
The Rayner-Slade Amalgamation
The Chestermarke Instinct
The Paradise Mystery
Dead Men's Money

Fergus Hume
The Mystery of a Hansom Cab
The Green Mummy
The Silent House
The Secret Passage

Edgar Jepson
The Loudwater Mystery

A. E. W. Mason
At the Villa Rose

A. A. Milne
The Red House Mystery
Baroness Emma Orczy
The Old Man in the Corner

Edgar Allan Poe
The Detective Stories of Edgar Allan Poe

Arthur J. Rees
The Hampstead Mystery
The Shrieking Pit
The Hand In The Dark
The Moon Rock
The Mystery of the Downs

Mary Roberts Rinehart
Sight Unseen and The Confession

Dorothy L. Sayers
Whose Body?

Sir William Magnay
The Hunt Ball Mystery

Mabel and Paul Thorne
The Sheridan Road Mystery

Raoul Whitfield
Death in a Bowl

And much more!
Visit ResurrectedPress.com
for our complete catalogue

About Resurrected Press

A division of Intrepid Ink, LLC, Resurrected Press is dedicated to bringing high quality, vintage books back into publication. See our entire catalogue and find out more at www.ResurrectedPress.com.

For announcements and updates on upcoming publications, LIKE us on Facebook!

www.Facebook.com/ResurrectedPress